ON THE BACKS OF OTHERS

ON THE BACKS OF OTHERS

ANDREW CROFTS

First published in Great Britain in 2025 by
Andrew Crofts, in partnership with whitefox publishing

www.wearewhitefox.com

ISBN 978-1-917523-10-3
Also available as an eBook
ISBN 978-1-917523-11-0

Designed and typeset by seagulls.net
Cover design by Ahlawat Gunjan
Project management by Whitefox Publishing Ltd

*For Susan, Alex, Amy, Livs, Jess, John,
Tom, Rosie, Phoebe, Gus and Beau.*

CHAPTER ONE

'I assume this charming message is meant for me.' Mrs Woodcock waved the creased cardboard she had ripped from the greenhouse door under Benson's dripping nose. Rotter opened one resentful eye, but didn't lift his head from the patch of warm sunlight he had found on the cracked cement.

Benson did not look up from his tomato plants, or signify that he had heard her. The sign had been up for so long he had stopped noticing it.

'He says you need to come,' she said, spinning the card onto the floor. The words 'BUGGER OFF', scrawled in marker pen, stared up at her from the chaos of broken pots and cobwebs. 'The man I told you about. The one who phoned. He's here now. He says it concerns both of us.'

Benson gave a rasping cough as he straightened up, expelling a large slug of phlegm into the pile of potting compost under the bench.

'Take your boots off before you come inside,' she added, as she walked out without looking back. 'And that disgusting dog stays outside.'

Rotter closed his eye and sank back into the peace and quiet of his dreams.

Benson took his time following Mrs Woodcock back to the house and made a pantomime of pulling off his boots at the door. He never wanted her to get the idea she could order him about, although she undoubtedly did, and by the time he joined them in the library the elderly visitor was showing signs of impatience that even a lifetime of studied politeness could not completely suppress. Seeing the state of the old gardener's socks as he shuffled across her polished floor for the first time in many years, beneath the towering glass-fronted mahogany bookcases, Mrs Woodcock decided it would have been wiser to have allowed him to keep his boots on. His dishevelled appearance was a stark contrast to the sharp creases of their visitor's pin-striped suit, the glowing whiteness of his collar and cuffs and the shiny gold of the cufflinks.

For a second, she was distracted by a movement at the window, but when she went over to check, there was no one there, just ragged trails of wisteria shifting in the breeze. By the time she turned back, Benson had made a show of making himself comfortable in the other wing-back leather chair and she only just managed to stop herself from scolding him for showing such disrespect in the circumstances. Even seeing him in this room fanned the coals of painful childhood jealousy, still smouldering somewhere deep inside her. She told herself that he had as much right to sit there as anyone else, but in her heart she didn't believe it.

The visitor gave Benson a curt nod of acknowledgement, to which Benson did not bother to respond. 'This concerns both of you equally,' he said, as what sounded like a small dog started yapping frantically from somewhere outside the house. 'It is rather a delicate matter.'

· · ·

When the dapper old man had appeared in the village the previous evening, the bar at the Crown Inn already contained the usual cheerful herd of local drinkers, all of whom fell silent and turned their heads as one as the creaking front door heralded the arrival of the second stranger of the evening. The smells of cooking mingled with those of centuries of spilled beer, overlaid with notes from the ash that had lain in the unlit fireplace all summer. There were faded hunting prints on the walls, but the lighting was too low to make out any of the bucolic details. Several of the light fittings lacked working bulbs and their shades had been knocked to precarious angles by the passing shoulders of drinkers. Everyone in the village liked it that way.

The first stranger, who had walked through the same door a few hours earlier, was already halfway through her light supper, sitting alone at a table in one of the darkest corners of the bar. For a second it seemed to the more hawk-eyed of the drinkers that the two of them exchanged glances of recognition. But if they did, the moment passed in the wink of an eye. The French woman, who had given her name to the landlady as Daisy de Courcy, returned to spearing her salad, which was constructed entirely from produce grown around the village. The sweetness of the tomatoes, on the brink of becoming overripe, compensated pleasantly for the bitterness of the sharply ridged peel on the cucumber.

A few late-summer petals from the pub garden had been scattered over the top. The old man made his way slowly to the bar, careful not to trip on the uneven stone floor, placing his cases down with fussy precision.

'Good evening,' he said to Joan, who was watching his approach from behind the bar. Her smile was the professional welcome of a landlady, her eyes suggesting a curiosity at finding two of her usually vacant bedrooms filled simultaneously. 'My name is Gerald Remers, I booked a room.'

'I know,' Joan said, as the rest of the room stayed silent and pretended not to be listening. The name had rung a dim and distant bell in her memory at the time the reservation was made, but she still couldn't think why that would be. Nothing about his appearance seemed familiar.

'I'm sorry to arrive so late. Is there any chance of getting something to eat?'

'We can probably rustle up something. What do you fancy?'

Having ordered a bowl of soup and a glass of wine, Gerald shuffled to a table at the opposite end of the room from the French woman and pointedly studied some papers from his time-worn briefcase, making it clear he did not wish to be engaged in conversation by anyone else in the room. Heads turned back towards Daisy, who was equally engrossed in reading something on an iPad, the landlady's dog curled contentedly beside her. Since nothing else of interest appeared to be imminent, the drinkers returned to the normal evening exchanges of village news, and views, peppered with the banter of people who had known one another a long time, as if the two strangers had now rendered themselves invisible.

An hour later, both visitors had actually disappeared, up to their bedrooms. As she sat at the dressing table, carefully removing her make-up, Daisy could hear the voices rising clearly through the dark, time-polished floorboards from the bar below.

'Did you see her handbag?' a younger voice asked Joan.

'I saw she had one …' Joan sounded like she was shrugging.

'Hermès,' the girl informed her.

'Which means?'

'Thousands and thousands of pounds.'

'Should be able to pay her bill then.'

'That coat was Chanel,' another female voice joined in.

'All a bit fancy for us, then.'

Daisy pictured Joan giving the bar a cursory wipe with the cloth she seemed to wear as a permanent accessory over her shoulder.

'Trotsky gave her the seal of approval,' Joan said, and Daisy assumed she meant the dog.

'Probably liked the way she smelled,' someone suggested.

'That was Chanel too.'

'It looked to me like they knew each other,' someone else ventured, and Daisy paused to listen more carefully, her fingertips lifting the skin on her cheeks, removing several more years from her reflection.

'You think they're having an illicit affair?'

'At his age?'

'Here?'

'What's wrong with here?' Joan asked, with an edge of genuine indignation in her voice.

'Well, it's not exactly the Ritz, is it?'

'They'll be waking up to some of the best views in England, I'll have you know. It was good enough for Victoria and Albert.'

'Still got the same plumbing as well.'

There was laughter and what sounded like a slap from Joan's wet tea-towel. Daisy returned to her nightly skincare routine as the conversation continued below her feet.

'Give us another round, Joanie.'

'The old boy looked like he was dressed more for a funeral than an affair.'

'You got a funeral on tomorrow, Vicar?'

'Nothing booked in. Maybe one of the other villages.'

'Didn't you ask either of them why they were here, Joanie?'

'None of my business,' Joan sniffed.

'How old do you reckon she is?'

'I know how old she is.' It was Joan's voice again. 'She showed me her passport when she arrived. She's in her seventies.'

'Seventies?' a chorus of shocked voices exclaimed, and Daisy smiled into the mirror as she applied a liberal quantity of La Mer to compensate her complexion for the rigors of the day's travels.

• • •

The misty valley view she awoke to the next morning was just as beautiful and expansive as Joan had predicted. The only sound to be heard was horses' hooves on the high street tarmac as the first ponies of the day were taken out for gentle exercise from the neighbouring livery yard. By the time Daisy got downstairs, Gerald was already halfway through his cooked breakfast. They nodded an acknowledgement of one another's existence as fellow travellers, giving no clue as to whether the drinkers' suspicions were well founded or not, and Daisy passed him on her way to the far end of the room. Watching from the kitchen, Joan paid closer attention to her guest's clothes, being more interested than she had wanted anyone to know the previous evening. Even with simple black trousers, black polo neck, and boots designed to look like they might have been inspired by something to do with riding, she could see that everything Daisy was wearing was expensive and carefully put together. She glanced down at her own comfortable, well-worn jeans and sweatshirt, and sighed.

'Where is Trotsky this morning?' Daisy asked.

'He's having a lie-in,' Joan said, as she poured her guest a cup of coffee. 'He's not as young as he was.'

'May I take him for a walk later?'

'Of course, he would love that. You need to keep him on a lead though, or you'll lose him down a rabbit hole. If he picks up a scent, he forgets he isn't a puppy anymore.'

'Okay.' Daisy laughed and held up her iPad to show a map of the village. 'Can you show me the best route? If this is the pub here, what's that building?'

'Oh, that's the big house,' Joan said, squinting at the map, 'it's all private round there. They don't like anyone walking through their land. There have been a few nasty incidents between ramblers and the gamekeeper over the years. You need to keep to the footpath round the side, outside the walls, that red dotted line. There are some lovely views over the valley.'

'The gamekeeper?' Daisy kept her voice casual. 'They have shooting there?'

'Not formal shoots. Not anymore. But you hear shooting now and then. Hunting rabbits, maybe, or keeping the foxes away from the chickens. They used to raise a lot of pheasants but I think the foxes wiped them out. They used to have peacocks too, but the foxes got them as well. As kids we used to follow them around the grounds for hours, just waiting for them to open their tails. Mind you, they made a god-awful racket, screeching at one another from the rooftops.'

Once Joan had disappeared into the kitchen with her breakfast order, Daisy went back to studying the map, switching to street view so she could track along the wall that surrounded the estate, looking for any openings that might allow her to slip through without triggering cameras. Judging by the density of the undergrowth inside the wall, she doubted that there were any or, if there were, that they would be working, but it never hurt to be careful. Where she came from, surveillance cameras were as standard as alarms and high gates for every large house, and most of the smaller ones.

• • •

An hour and a half later, Gerald was setting off from the pub, slowly and cautiously, avoiding the potholes as he headed towards the weed-covered gates of the big house in preparation for the long walk up the drive to the front door, while Daisy strolled as discreetly as she could manage, with Trotsky whirling around her ankles in tight circles of excitement, along the road at the back, following the outer wall of the estate. Most of the ancient stones were swamped in a thick mat of dark-green ivy; home, no doubt, to untold thousands of small creatures. The tangled, spiky tentacles of the brambles sprouted from stems as thick as the branches of small trees. The verge was so overgrown, Daisy almost missed the hole in the wall that she had spotted on Google. Clambering over the fallen stones, dislodged by a carelessly driven car sometime in the past, she gave up trying to avoid scuffing her boots, as the thick undergrowth forced her to stumble on virtually every step. Struggling to stay upright, she noticed a smear of blood on her palm, but the mission was too important for her to fret about such small stuff. Trotsky pulled hard on the lead, sensing the possibility of escape and independent adventure, giving Daisy no time to avoid the bramble tendrils that scraped her face and grabbed at her clothing as she forced her way forward.

Eventually regaining her equilibrium, she reined the dog in with some ferocity, rebalancing the power structure between them. Trotsky accepted her authority cheerfully, but immediately went back to pulling in the direction of interesting trails, ignoring the restrictions of the collar, which had tightened around his throat, making him cough and wheeze constantly as he wriggled enthusiastically onwards.

There was a rustle in the brambles, and a flash of red fur, as a fox made a dash for safety.

After what seemed like an age, the walls of the house loomed up through the undergrowth, just a few feet away, and she hauled Trotsky in. He looked up at her as if sensing something interesting was about to happen and awaiting an order. Peering through the branches, she could see that this had once been the back elevation of the house, no doubt looking out over sweeping lawns, which had since reverted to the jungle she had just battled through. The tall, elegant windows were barely visible amidst the bundles of wisteria hanging off rusty fixings, which bound their gnarled, twisting stems to the brickwork. Only one downstairs window was not barred from prying eyes by wooden shutters. Daisy crouched low, lifting a wriggling Trotsky under her arm, and crept closer. Raising her head slowly over the froth of wisteria leaves, she peered in.

As her eyes adjusted to the darkness inside, she could make out the back of a wing-back leather chair, with Gerald's pin-striped sleeve and white cuff resting on the arm. Two other people were in the room, who she guessed were the ones she was looking for. As Mrs Woodcock seemed for a split second to glance in her direction, Daisy ducked down and ran in a crouch round the corner of the house, where the windows were less grand and less firmly shuttered. One casement stood slightly open. Daisy tied Trotsky to a sturdy buddleia, which had rooted itself firmly into a crack in the courtyard's brick floor, and pulled the window fully open. With an agility honed by many a Pilates class, she pulled herself up onto the sill and dropped down into a room that smelled of a mixture of cleaning products and damp washing. There was a single bed, neatly made up, in the corner of the room. Pausing for a second to check that she could not hear any movements or voices on the other side of the door, Daisy let herself into the deserted kitchen and set off on her search for a staircase to the bedrooms. She could hear Gerald's fragile voice through a closed door, explaining the situation. Trotsky was yapping impatiently for her to return and release him. The tempting scent of the nearby foxes was almost more than he could bear.

CHAPTER TWO

By the evening, Gerald had checked out from the pub, complimenting Joan on the 'traditional charm' of her 'establishment' as a chauffeur held open the door of a gleamingly clean black Mercedes. Daisy almost blended into the background, like a regular fixture, as she ate her daily salad and listened to the gossip swirling round the bar. Although no one had yet succeeded in engaging her in any sort of conversation, beyond her short exchanges with Joan, the drinkers had grown almost used to her silent presence, and didn't seem to mind what she overheard, any more than they minded Trotsky's constantly pricked ears and watchful eyes. She was obviously a woman who kept herself to herself, and they all respected that, even the ones who found it hard to follow the same practice themselves. Joan had noted the scratches on her guest's face when she returned from her walk, but those had since vanished in the dimly lit room, beneath skilfully applied concealer.

'He's died? How do you know?' A voice at the next table caught Daisy's attention, but she kept her eyes on her plate and her iPad.

'My cleaner's daughter is in the police. She answered the call.'

'I thought he died years ago.'

'He must have been at least ninety.'

'Do they really call the police when an old bloke in his nineties drops dead?'

'Apparently, they have to come out if the deceased hasn't been seen recently by a doctor.'

'Is that right, Doctor?'

'Something like that,' one of the local doctors confirmed from a stool at the bar.

'I thought I heard sirens a few days ago. They must have been going up to the house.'

'So, were there suspicious circumstances? Did she say?'

'She said everything about the place was suspicious. She said it was like a film set for an Agatha Christie, or maybe a Hammer horror. She said something about a gun, but then she clammed up. I think she was worried she had said too much.'

'No wonder the police came, if there was a gun involved.'

'I've often heard shots. Thought they were shooting pigeons or something.'

'I bet the whole place is in a right state. A mate of mine was called in to deal with some holes in the roof a few years ago, and he said it was bad then. There's been nothing done up there since his old man died.'

'When was that, then?' a young voice asked.

'Back in the eighties some time. It was immaculate in those days. I remember my dad taking me up to watch the hunt meeting on the front lawn, all the toffs out in their red coats …'

'Pink coats,' someone interrupted, 'they called them "pink".'

'Whatever. They'd be quaffing down the port and hee-hawing at one another. The horses would be churning up the grass something terrible, but the Colonel didn't mind. The gardeners would have the whole thing rolled and reseeded within a couple of weeks. He loved those horses, looked after them like they were his children.'

'He was a cavalry officer, wasn't he, in the War?'

'Involved in the liberation of Paris, I heard. Bit of a hero, working under cover for Churchill.'

'The hunt was exciting for us kids.'

'It was a great social occasion. It brought the village together.'

'The Colonel kept that hunt going single-handedly.'

'His lad ended it, didn't he?'

'Nobody knew quite what happened. There were lots of rumours.'

'Do you remember how the hounds used to howl in the night? It was hard to sleep sometimes.'

'When I was a kid, I used to think it was wolves.'

'Then one day they just stopped. Complete silence. It seemed weird.'

'Good riddance, I say. The unspeakable in pursuit of the uneatable, isn't that what they say?'

'It was a wonderful sight though, when they were in full swing, pouring across the fields and over the hedges.'

'Through the hedges, more like. I was forever having to patch them up after they'd been out. Half of them couldn't jump to save their lives, weekend riders, just ploughed straight through.'

'The hounds could make a right mess if they got into a garden too.'

'Now it's the foxes that mess up the beds, digging for worms and whatnot, leaving their deposits on the lawns.'

There were chuckles from the darker corners of the bar, where some of the older voices were emanating from.

'One of them buried an egg in my border. Found it the other day.'

'Must have stolen it from a doorstep. I get the milkman to leave my delivery in a box.'

'My old man went up to the house to complain once that the hounds had been through his herbaceous border, so the Colonel marched him down to the greenhouses, got the gardeners to load up a couple of wheelbarrows of plants and restocked the whole bed for him.'

'He knew how to look after people.'

'He helped your mum a lot in here after your dad died, didn't he, Joanie?'

'I don't really remember,' Joan said, without looking up from the glass she was polishing. 'I was too young.'

A man at the bar opened his mouth as if to take issue with her, then caught her eye and thought better of it.

'Who's been living up there since the eighties, then?' someone young asked.

'According to my mum,' an older voice answered, 'only the Colonel's son, the one who you say just snuffed it, and the couple who were supposed to be looking after him.'

'Did the police think they'd done him in?'

'They're not saying if they do or they don't.'

'Who will inherit? Are there any children?'

'Oh no,' an elderly voice gave a dry laugh, 'there won't be any children in there.'

The voices stopped and the heads turned as the hinges on the door to the courtyard creaked. The door hesitated, as if someone was having second thoughts, and the whole room held its breath, watching as the heavy slabs of once polished oak moved a few more inches, scraping across the flagstones just far enough to allow the two dishevelled figures to squeeze through. The silence followed them all the way to the bar, and even Daisy was unable to resist looking up. Rotter slunk through the door between their legs and into the shadow of the bar, where he lay down slowly, with stiffened joints, ignoring Trotsky's following stare.

'Guinness,' Benson said, once they reached the waiting landlady.

'Scotch, please,' Mrs Woodcock added, and Joan didn't bother to ask her which one.

It was like the curtain had just gone up and the audience were waiting eagerly to see what the performers were going to do next. Everyone watched as the Guinness crept from the pump to the glass, all eyes on Joan's reddened knuckles as she started and stopped the flow with a skill honed over a lifetime.

'So,' Joan broke the silence on everyone's behalf once Benson and Mrs Woodcock had received and paid for their drinks with coins dug from deep in their coat pockets, and Benson had helped himself to some dog treats from the jar, dropping them beside Rotter's sleeping, drooling face, 'are you from the big house?'

'Yes.' Mrs Woodcock emptied her glass in three swift movements, placing it down on the bar and nodding for a refill of Dutch courage.

'I was sorry to hear of your loss,' Joan ventured, and someone at the back of the room let out a small snorting sound, which might have been a suppressed laugh, a small show of derision, or possibly an unexpected sneeze.

Mrs Woodcock nodded her acceptance of the condolence. Neither she nor Benson moved away from the bar. Daisy's eyes flickered around the various faces as they watched from the shadows, waiting while she paid for her second drink.

'Thank you,' she said, aware that her bar chat with the landlady was in reality a declaration to the whole village community. 'We miss him.'

Benson let out a derisive coughing noise, depositing the resulting phlegm in a piece of rag from his pocket that might once have been a handkerchief.

'Will the house go up for sale?' Joan asked.

'It is a little complicated,' Mrs Woodcock said, glancing warningly at Benson, who now had a moustache of froth from the Guinness. 'Bryan was not very good with money.'

Several people exchanged knowing looks. It was a well-known cliché, the 'old retainers' who took advantage of a vulnerable employer, draining him of his money as he gradually lost his grip on reality. If the money had run out, there would be no reason for them to keep him alive any longer. Case solved.

'Apparently there are just debts, which now belong to a property development company, who have plans to turn the estate into a holiday centre.'

'What kind of holiday centre?' someone asked.

'Caravans.' Benson spat the word into the room like a bullet. 'Hundreds of them. All round the grounds.'

The wall of silence was broken by a surge of horrified exclamations, some of them surprisingly profane for a family establishment.

'So, who has he left the house and the estate to?' Joan asked as the noise settled back to an attentive silence.

'Us.' Mrs Woodcock glanced again at Benson, who shrugged and licked the foam from his moustache with a nicotine-stained tongue. 'He's left the debts to us. We thought you should all know, as the community that would be affected by any changes.'

'Like a caravan site,' Benson reminded them.

'Who are you exactly?' someone wanted to know.

'We've lived on the estate all our lives,' Mrs Woodcock said. 'We were both born there.'

Daisy sat as still as a birdwatcher confronted by a flock of rare and shy specimens, desperate not to remind anyone of her presence as an eavesdropper.

'A caravan site?' someone said, as the possible consequences of what they were hearing sank further into the collective consciousness.

'Hundreds and hundreds of them,' Benson reiterated, for emphasis.

'You need to rent the house out,' a voice suggested.

'We live there,' Mrs Woodcock snapped. 'I told you.'

'You don't live in every room, do you?' Joan's tone was equally impatient.

'Open it to the public,' someone suggested, and several voices agreed, all more than happy to pay the price of admittance for a chance to see what had been going on behind the brambles for so many years.

'You could Airbnb some of the bedrooms,' another voice chimed in.

'What's that?' Mrs Woodcock asked.

'Bed and breakfast on the internet, although there's no breakfast involved. That way you can just let out the rooms, if you don't want to cook.'

'There hasn't been a decent cook in the house for more than thirty years,' Benson grunted, passing his empty glass back to Joan and nodding for a refill.

'I cooked every day for Bryan,' Mrs Woodcock sniffed, 'and you were always happy enough to eat anything he didn't.'

'Beggars can't be choosers,' Benson continued to mutter, pleased to see that several people around the bar were finding his contributions to the drama amusing.

'Or turn it into a wedding venue,' Joan suggested, reluctant to encourage anyone to compete with her own, virtually non-existent bed and breakfast trade. 'My daughter, Molly, is a wedding planner down in London. I could ask her to come and have a look, if you like.'

'A wedding planner?' Mrs Woodcock looked puzzled by the concept.

'Rich people, celebrities, those types,' Joan explained,

although she was unsure herself of exactly how her daughter earned her living. 'They hire someone to organise their whole wedding, including finding a venue. Some of them spend a fortune, apparently.'

'What would we have to do?' Benson sounded suspicious, wary that he was being lured into some sort of trap.

'I don't think you have to do anything, beyond letting them use the house and grounds for a few days, and then you pocket the fee. Molly's the one to talk to. I'll ring her when we've closed up, if you're interested.'

'Thank you.' Mrs Woodcock was deliberately avoiding the deathstare Benson was aiming at the back of her head.

Daisy googled wedding planners in London called Molly.

CHAPTER THREE

The following day, Molly glided into the pub car park in the brand-new Range Rover that she had recently leased, for monthly payments substantially larger than the exorbitant rent she paid for her cupboard of a flat in London, because she knew her clients expected her to be able to afford it. Personally, she had been happier buzzing around in the ancient Mini she had inherited from her mother when she left home, but her clients found such parsimony entirely counter-intuitive, and judged the value of her services accordingly. Appearances, it seemed, were everything when you were trying to sell anything to the rich.

It was lunchtime in the pub and her arrival raised a cheer from the regulars. Several of them, who had known Molly all her life, insisted on buying her drinks before she and her mother were due to go up to the big house to inspect its potential as a venue. Trotsky whirled with excitement at the scent of his old friend as she knelt down to greet him, her bracelets jangling as he rolled and squirmed happily in her strong fingers, honed by a childhood spent controlling large horses. Daisy listened from her usual table as the crowd interrogated Molly about her famous clients and their tantalisingly shocking 'bridezilla' demands, most of which did not sound particularly shocking to Daisy after many years living amongst the grande dames and the young Russian wives who haunted the Riviera.

By the time Joan let everyone know that she was closing up to go to the big house, Molly was sufficiently inebriated not to protest when virtually everyone in the bar decided to come with her on her inspection tour.

'My cousin just got engaged,' one person announced, as a justification for their interest. 'They've been looking for a venue for the wedding.'

'I could talk about the house on my Instagram,' another suggested. 'A lot of my followers are planning their weddings at the moment.'

'My sister-in-law down the road had years of catering experience on yachts in the Mediterranean, before she started having children, and I know she's thinking of going back to work …'

'The dogs need to stretch their legs.'

By the time Molly and Joan set off, they had a party of nearly twenty people accompanying them on the long walk down the potholed drive, many of them with their spirits warmed by more lunchtime drinks than they might normally have allowed themselves, along with half a dozen equally eager dogs. Everyone was so distracted by the revelation of the wilderness state of the once immaculate landscape surrounding them that they didn't take any notice of Daisy, who had joined the back of the crowd without bothering to make up an excuse, as if it were perfectly natural for her to be taking a pleasant stroll after her lunchtime quiche. Trotsky could hardly believe his luck at having so many of his friends accompanying him across what was, for him, virgin territory. Villagers had been banned from coming up the drive many years before any of their dogs had been born.

'The village fêtes always used to be held on the lawns somewhere over there,' Joan informed her daughter, and anyone else within earshot, waving vaguely towards a dense thicket of woodland. 'They were huge events. People came from all the surrounding villages, several hundred of them some years. There were marquees, coconut shies, cream teas, donkey rides, everything.'

'Master Bryan never showed his face though, did he?' someone within earshot reminded her.

'I only really remember his father being there,' another agreed.

'His mother would do the rounds sometimes, being the gracious lady.'

'That was her name, wasn't it, Grace?'

'Lady Grace.'

'Very elegant, but a bit toffee-nosed.'

'She never came down the pub with him, did she?'

'It was her money keeping the whole place going, as far as I can remember.'

'That's what people always said,' Joan agreed. 'I don't know how they thought they knew whose money it was. I doubt anyone had a conversation with them about their finances. The Colonel must have made a packet when they sold off the farms.'

'Mind you, it must have cost them a fair bit to pay off your dad, eh Joan?' someone teased.

'Not something he ever liked to talk about,' Joan said, her tone suggesting she didn't intend to talk about it either.

'He knew how to drink, did the Colonel. My goodness, he could put it away.'

'He bought a fair few rounds too. He was generous, I'll say that for him. Never got a round out of his son.'

'Never saw the boy in the pub, that I can remember.'

'How's your mum doing these days, Joanie?' someone else asked.

'Not too bad, thanks for asking.'

'I keep meaning to drop in, but I don't know if she would remember me.'

'Probably not,' Joan said, 'but she'd still love a visit. Some days she remembers more than others.'

'I remember being taken to children's Christmas parties in their front hall,' someone changed the subject back to memories of the big house. 'Her Ladyship would have presents for all of us, all beautifully wrapped, and then the old man, dressed as Father Christmas, would give each of the mothers a glass of sherry.'

'You were lucky if that was all he gave you,' one of the older women muttered, making her walking companion chuckle knowingly.

'The whole village ran like clockwork when they were alive.'

'They must be spinning in their graves to see the state the house is in now.'

'It's such a shame.'

'So much potential,' Molly murmured, ignoring the chattering of the elderly voices surrounding her, as she swung her phone round to film. 'I can't believe I was living next to this place all through my childhood, and never plucked up the courage to come over the wall. We used to make up stories about who lived here, "behind the wild wood". An angry giant maybe, who would eat trespassing children for his tea, or a witch who had put a spell round the place so no one could get in.' She turned to take in the following crowd. 'Who's the chic French lady at the back?'

'She's staying at the pub,' Joan said.

'But who is she?'

'No idea. She hasn't talked to anyone.'

'Does she speak English?'

'Seems to.'

'She just booked a room and moved into the village without giving you any idea why?'

Joan nodded.

'Is she on holiday?'

'She's been getting post delivered to her at the pub, so I guess she's expecting to stay a while. That's all I know. Truly.'

Molly laughed. 'You're slipping. I thought you knew everything about everyone.'

'Yeah, well, usually,' Joan said. 'We had another mystery guest the other night too. This really old man in a pin-striped suit and tie. Don't know what he was up to either.'

'Is he still with you?'

'No. He only stayed one night. It looked like they might know each other, but they didn't let on.'

'You mean, like they were having a secret affair?'

'That's what Betty said. I don't think so. You should have seen him. He was about ninety years old.'

'It's been known, Mum. This is the age of Viagra, after all.'

'Hmm. Maybe. But anyway, he's gone now, and she's still here.'

'And these two old retainers at the big house just turned up out of nowhere as well?'

'Sort of. There are people who say they know who they are, or at least who they were. A few of the oldies remember their parents. Apparently, they worked up at the house too, when the Colonel was still around. These two haven't been seen in the village for at least ten years, maybe twenty, unless they were driving somewhere in the Colonel's old Bentley, and they certainly haven't been into the pub, until last night.'

'Wow!' Molly exclaimed, raising her phone to resume filming as they rounded the final bend of the drive. 'Look at that!'

The gaggle of villagers paused to gaze in awe at the big house as it rose up out of the tangled woodland that had once been its gardens. Twenty-foot-high columns framed the steps up to the French doors. The panes of glass that weren't broken and boarded over glinted in the low afternoon sun, giving the building the air of a stage set waiting for a drama to restart. A pair of foxes appeared from the undergrowth onto the drive and froze, staring at the pack of dogs for a few moments before disappearing. None of the dogs seemed to have noticed.

CHAPTER FOUR

'No, no, no!' Mrs Woodcock stood four-square in the doorway, arms spread wide, barring entry to her domain. 'No dogs in the house. I've just polished the floor. Boots and shoes off, please. Thank you.'

All eyes immediately slid to the sweeping vista of polished oak parquet that glowed behind her, golden brown in the afternoon sunbeams.

'You do all this yourself?' someone asked in awe as they fumbled to remove their footwear, hopping amongst the writhing, bickering mass of dogs.

'Have to,' Mrs Woodcock said with a shrug. 'Everyone else is dead and gone now. It was my mother's pride and joy, but she had a couple of maids to help her. Once they retired, Bryan didn't want anyone new in the house. He was used to me, and he liked the way I worked. He always said no one could make these floors shine like I did.'

'I'm not surprised. It looks fabulous.'

'How do you find the time?'

'Don't waste my days watching television or reading books, or drinking and gossiping in the pub,' she said. 'You'd be surprised what you can get done in a day, if you just get on with it. I like to keep busy. Keeps your mind from dwelling on things.'

'It all looks amazing,' Molly cooed, filming the grand staircase, which she could imagine her clients descending in clouds of silk and lace. There was one in particular, Zahara, who she was pretty sure would love the *Downton Abbey* vibe. 'Quite a few repairs needed—' she gestured towards the boarded panes in the doors '—and the grounds need some attention.'

'Benson has been having some trouble with his knees,' Mrs Woodcock said, 'and his back. And his attitude. He is not the man his father was, before he had the stroke, that is. Spends a good deal too much time sat on his backside, with his nose buried in a book. You would never have caught his father, or mine, doing that when there was so much work to be done around the place.'

'I remember old Mr Benson,' an elderly villager piped up. 'He used to give us kids rides with his tractor and trailer on fête days.'

'Rolled the whole thing over one year,' another voice remembered. 'On the bank down by the lake. Kids flying every which way. There were a couple of broken arms, I seem to remember. The Colonel thought it was hilarious. Drove them to the hospital himself, in that Bentley of his.'

'Wouldn't be able to do that now. Health and safety.'

There was a general mumble of agreement.

'What about Mr Woodcock?' Joan asked, ignoring her daughter's shocked expression at the sudden injection of such a personal question. 'Does he live here?'

Mrs Woodcock pulled herself up at least another three inches. 'He died more than twenty years ago ...'

'Oh,' Joan said, 'I'm sorry.'

'He was born here too, and married my mother here in nineteen fifty two. She and Benson's mother were born in another cottage on the estate. They were sisters.'

Joan tried again. 'I meant your husband.'

'Oh, no. My father was the last Mr Woodcock to live here.'

'But your name. I thought you said …'

'When I became housekeeper, it seemed more appropriate to be seen as a married woman. It was a tradition and the Colonel and Her Ladyship liked keeping up traditions, and Bryan thought it would be more seemly. There's been Woodcocks working in this house for more than two hundred years. My father was a joiner by trade. He built most of the stables himself and the greenhouses. He was a real craftsman, learned it from his father.'

Molly's camera had swung round to a painting stretching at least fifteen feet above the entrance, up towards the vaulted ceiling of the hall. It depicted two elegant people, a man and a woman, in formal hunting gear, sitting regally on their horses, with hounds milling round the horses' legs. Daisy had slipped past the crowd and was standing at the back of the room, staring up at the picture. At a moment when everyone was distracted, she took out her phone and snapped a picture of the portrait.

'Impressive picture,' Molly said.

'That's the old Colonel and his wife, Lady Grace,' Joan told her. 'They were a good-looking couple, when they were in their prime.'

'Their boy was good-looking too,' someone added, 'too good-looking for his own good, as it turned out.'

Joan turned back to Mrs Woodcock and opened her mouth to make further enquiries but Molly's face suggested she had already trespassed too far into the housekeeper's personal territory. Mrs Woodcock's expression seemed to have grown even more impenetrably stony than before, as if she felt she had been tricked into saying more than she meant to. The villagers, having secured their disgruntled dogs to the balustrades outside, were now dispersing around the house while they had the chance, sliding in their stockinged feet, in a variety of directions, making it hard for Mrs Woodcock to keep an eye on all of them as they scattered through different rooms, exchanging whispered opinions and speculations as they went.

'You really keep this whole place going on your own?' Molly, who had trouble keeping her one-bedroom flat in Peckham from smelling like a week-old kitchen bin, was genuinely shocked. 'Wow! Respect!'

Two gunshots echoed in through the open front door, followed by angry, panicked barking from the tethered dogs.

'What was that?' Molly asked.

'He'll be shooting pigeons off the roof,' Mrs Woodcock said.

'Who will?'

'Tom Benson. He's partial to pigeon pie.'

'The gardener has a gun?'

'Gardener. Gamekeeper. Handyman, chauffeur, Jack of all trades, master of none. He used to be a pretty good shot. Not as good as his father, mind, or the Colonel. Keeps the larder stocked with pigeon and rabbit, sometimes a pheasant or two if the foxes haven't got them first. He used to look after the chickens, but the foxes finished them off a while back. He brought in a full-sized deer one year, kept us going all through the winter.'

Several villagers reappeared through the doors. 'We heard gunshots,' one said.

'Do you want to see the rest of the house?' Mrs Woodcock asked Molly, as if they were the only two in the room.

'Definitely.'

She returned to filming as Mrs Woodcock led her, Joan, and anyone else who hadn't peeled off independently, through the dining room, library, drawing room and orangery. Everywhere the smell of polish mingled with the aromas of age that seeped from the books on the shelves, the canvases and tapestries on the walls, and the sun-bleached materials gathered at the windows and covering the chairs and sofas. Knowing they were coming, Mrs Woodcock had unbolted the shutters to allow the sunlight inside, even opening a couple of windows to permit the air to move. Anything that could be cleaned, from glass decanters to silver ornaments, shone from her attentions. The gold embossing on the spines of the books that lined the library walls gleamed inside the glass cabinets.

'Does anybody actually read all these books?' Joan asked. 'Or are they just for show?'

'I dare say someone read them once,' Mrs Woodcock sniffed. 'Like I said, I don't have time for reading. Never have had. Never will. I just dust them.'

Upstairs, the bedrooms had the same well-loved shine to them.

'The whole place has been cleaned, top to bottom,' one villager observed in a stage whisper.

'Like cleaning up a crime scene,' her friend agreed. 'That's what the gangsters do. Send in a professional cleaner who knows how to get rid of bloodstains and fingerprints.'

'Harvey Keitel,' someone added helpfully. 'The Wolf in *Pulp Fiction*.'

'Maybe she's just a really great housekeeper.'

'No one is this good. You would have to be polishing from dawn to dusk to stay on top of this pile.'

'What else has she got to do with her days?'

'Good point.'

'My clients would expect en-suite bathrooms,' Molly said, as they reached the tenth bedroom and she imagined Zahara's reaction to the idea of a shared bathroom, let alone Zahara's mother.

'Oh dear,' Mrs Woodcock replied.

The kitchen, which looked exactly as it had when it was installed in 1975, worried Molly less.

'We would bring in our own catering unit,' she explained, and Mrs Woodcock bit her lip.

'Would Benson mind if we had a look round the grounds?' Joan asked.

'Doesn't matter if he does. You'll probably find him with the vegetables in the walled garden.'

'Do you grow all your own fruit and veg then?' Molly asked.

'Yes, that's the one useful thing he does do.'

Mrs Woodcock heard the mother and daughter exchanging previously suppressed giggles as they went out the back door towards the walled garden. She rolled her eyes, dabbed away a tear that had taken her by surprise, and blew her nose with some violence. It was time to herd the gossiping villagers up and get them back out the door.

Benson was working in an orchard at the far corner of the walled garden, digging a hole between the roots of a plum tree. Rotter lay on the ground beside him, amongst the fallen plums. Half the beds were as overgrown as the rest of the estate, but as Molly and Joan drew closer to the orchard, they passed more recently tended rows of plants. The last of the raspberries were waiting to be picked from elaborate structures of canes on one side of the path, rows of overgrown lettuces, onions and cabbages awaited pulling on the other. Courgette plants were sprawling over the rotting wooden sleepers that edged the beds, and across the threadbare gravel. Neither Benson nor Rotter looked up as they approached. Molly tried to make her filming seem more discreet, although she wanted to get a record of the old man toiling in his beloved garden, knowing how much it would tickle Zahara's obsession with English class structures, and history. They had almost reached Benson before Joan noticed that the pool of redness around Rotter's head, which she had assumed was juice from the fallen plums, was actually blood. She let out an involuntary squeak.

'Your dog!' she said, assuming the old man had failed to notice the bleeding.

Benson sighed as, slowly and carefully, he straightened up from his digging, the stub of his skilfully rolled cigarette close to burning the lip it was stuck to.

'Your dog is bleeding.'

'He's dead,' Benson said, and returned to his grave-digging duties.

Joan and Molly fell silent as they tried to process what they were looking at, and it was then that they saw the shotgun resting in the wheelbarrow.

CHAPTER FIVE

'This is my absolute, best, best, best friend, Molly.' Zahara chatted as if there was someone else in the palatial pale-grey kitchen, apart from the two of them. To her, the camera on her phone was also a friend, a physical distillation of the several million people around the world who loved to hear everything she had to say about everything, at the same time as watching and admiring her physical perfection. They were her followers. Some might call them her fans, but she was far too self-effacing to use such a term. That would have been way too Bollywood, and not nearly as girl-next-door as she believed her brand to be. She assured them all the time that she thought of them as her friends, her extended family. That was how she made her posts sound so natural, like she was simply introducing one friend to another, one cousin to another. It also made her obvious wealth and privilege more palatable to the many who could never hope to experience anything like it for themselves, unless of course they went to work for families such as Zahara's.

Early in her startling rise to global popularity, she had heard an old radio star saying that the secret of successful broadcasting was to imagine that you were speaking to just one person. Then it would sound personal to everyone listening, even if there were millions of them, which there now were. Of course, they could see her too, which was why she always made a point of looking her best when the camera was on. It seemed only polite to make the maximum effort when in company.

In the past, Molly would never have described Zahara as a friend exactly, even though they had spent three years on the same design course. Zahara had been in many of the same lecture halls and studios as Molly, and sometimes even at the same time, but Molly could not recall a single occasion where they had socialised together. None of the people she would count as her actual friends from that period could remember Zahara being present at any social occasion. No one ever saw her drunk, or went to her home for a meal or to watch a movie. She was never in any of the groups that went on holiday together, unless it was a trip organised by a tutor, for educational purposes. Even on those trips, when everyone else met up in the evenings for eating or drinking sessions, or possibly even sex, Zahara was nowhere to be seen. Whether they were in Paris or Hong Kong, Dubai or Mumbai, she always seemed to have someone else to stay with, in a place that no one else would be privy to. When you looked and dressed like Zahara, you could get into places that normally discouraged penniless folk, such as design students. This lack of a social life with her peer group – Molly and her friends now agreed, when they occasionally met up to reminisce about their student days – was probably why Zahara was so fabulously successful, with millions of followers, while they were all back living with their parents, or sharing flats, or existing in single rooms in the recently gentrified areas of the ever more sprawling city, with online friendship groups in the mere hundreds rather than the millions.

'She's been living the billionaire lifestyle since the day she was born,' Molly had girlsplained to the group one evening, after they had crammed into her flat, an unhealthy number of bottles of wine having been consumed in a nearby restaurant. 'Why would she ever have been interested in our tawdry drinking sessions?'

'She doesn't drink anyway, does she?' someone added.

'Maybe champagne if it's an event, or a fancy cocktail if she has mixed it on camera, usually with someone famous.'

'I've never seen her take more than a sip, even then.'

'Mmmmm—' someone mimicked Zahara's ever-positive tones '—soooo delicious! I love, love, love it!'

'None of us was ever going to get up the courage to make a pass at such a total, physical goddess,' a male friend added, a little mournfully, from his supine position on the floor. 'So, there wouldn't have been much point hanging out with her.'

'That's a grim little glimpse into the male mind,' Molly said, giving him a kick from where she was sprawled on a bean bag.

'She didn't drink, didn't smoke, or do anything else,' said another. 'Which would have made her a bit of an atmosphere killer.'

'She was already a grown-up, when the rest of us were pretty much still overgrown schoolchildren. It was probably more interesting for her to work, and hang out with her family.'

'And network.'

'How could anything be more fun than hanging out with us?' the friend on the floor asked the whole room, as he scrabbled his way outside on all fours to throw up on Molly's communal terrace.

Although she felt no urge to be in their company, however, Zahara did follow all her student contemporaries on social media, which was how she came to see that Molly had set herself up as a wedding planner, and why she had got in touch with her offer of employment, an offer that came with instant best-friend status attached. Molly was more than happy to accept both offers, if only temporarily, and for as long as she could invoice monthly for her time. Since then, however, in the course of their many planning meetings, she had actually started to feel like she and Zahara might be friends after all. She had even grown used to thinking and talking in the sort of numbers Zahara and her family threw around so casually all the time. If something was going to be a few thousand pounds more than predicted, for instance, she now knew she did not need to bother to mention it. No one in the family even seemed to be that troubled when sums in the hundreds of thousands were tossed about.

'We have been doing some crazy, creative brainstorming,' Zahara was telling the millions who might be watching, her voice echoing off the cool, clear, pale-grey marble surfaces surrounding them. 'And laying plans for the wedding of the century. I've been working on some preliminary designs for the dress, which obviously we are going to be keeping top secret up to the big day, especially top secret from Carolyn.' She pressed her finger to her lips in an exaggerated gesture of silent discretion.

'And I have been doing some location scouting—' Molly picked up her cue like a pro, following Zahara's lead and talking to the camera on its stand, as if it was a person '—which has to be the most fun job ever.'

'The theme for the whole thing is going to be Jane Austen,' Zahara resumed talking, 'which is so totally English, and which is really annoying Mama.' She giggled and swung the camera round to show her mother, who had just appeared in the doorway, glowing against the grey walls in a scarlet and gold sari. Mama shrugged theatrically for the viewers, her expression an impenetrable mask, which made Zahara laugh even more, and made Molly squirm with discomfort. 'You love all that Mr Darcy stuff, Mama,' Zahara teased. 'You know you do. That wet shirt scene …'

Mama poured herself a coffee, with no change of expression. She knew how to play her role as straight man to her daughter's popular displays of almost respectful and always affectionate humour at her expense. She would save her own voice for the rare moments when the camera was turned off. Her daughter was generating a lot of money and that, in Mama's eyes, meant she deserved respect, even if she was not always as respectful a daughter as she should be. An equally expressionless dachshund stared up at her from the heated Italian floor tiles.

'Molly has been showing me film she took of the most divine house imaginable,' Zahara continued to camera. 'It's surrounded by wild, wild woodland, and we have such plans for transforming it into a magical wonderland for our guests. I am so looking forward to sharing with you guys what we are doing as we go along, and then to having you all there with me on the day. Not only is it going to be beautiful and magical, it is going to be the greenest, most climate-friendly project ever! More news soon!'

Zahara switched off her phone and squinted more carefully at Molly's phone screen, which was lying beside her, still silently playing the video from the house. 'Who's the old dude?'

'He's like one of the old retainers of the estate. Sort of a gardener-cum-gamekeeper.'

'Oh wow! That is so Lady Chatterley!'

'Not exactly a dashing romantic figure.'

'Is that a gun in the wheelbarrow?'

'He'd just had to put his dog down. It was really sad, actually.'

'He shot his dog? Wow, that's so gothic!'

'Old country folk have their ways, you know. They don't tend to be sentimental about things like life and death. See too much of it, I guess. Nature being "red in tooth and claw", that sort of thing.'

Molly remembered the matter-of-fact way that her grandfather had shot her first pony when he became too exhausted to even stand up anymore. She had tried her best to hide her tears from the rest of the family, and now she thought back to the event with the benefit of passing time, she did wonder why no one thought to give her a comforting hug. The memory made her swallow hard.

'Yeah. No. Really, it's not a problem,' Zahara said. 'It's totally authentic. I like it. It makes me think he's a man you can trust. Oh my God, I can feel real tears coming.' She fanned her eyes theatrically with long, delicate, intensely manicured and intricately hennaed fingers, fearful of getting too close and smudging her mascara.

'He and the housekeeper seem to have been incredibly loyal to their employer all their lives,' Molly said, managing to overcome the catch in her throat. 'It's kind of spooky, to be honest.'

'That is so Jane Austen, so *Jane Eyre*, so Daphne du Maurier. I love it. Servants being loyal to their masters and respecting their traditions. How often do you get that sort of thing in this day and age? I love it!'

'It could cost quite a bit to lick the place into shape after so many years of neglect …'

'We can get the sponsors involved. They'll love it. Soooo English! Soooo authentic! We can make a documentary of the renovation. People love a "before-and-after" thing. And Daddy will help. His people can renovate anything in no time at all. They put up whole tower blocks in Shanghai and Dubai almost overnight. Do you want to see my preliminary sketches for the dress?'

'Sure. What about Carolyn? What will she be wearing?'

'I thought we could go with the classic Lord Byron look for her: romantic, long black frock coat, big, high collar, tight britches to show off her long legs, and mix that with the classic St Laurent tux. Marlene Dietrich, Audrey Hepburn … you know the kind of thing. So elegant, so simple, such clean lines.'

'Is she up for that?'

'She couldn't care less,' Zahara grimaced. 'She is more than happy to leave it all to me. She knows that I want to make her look fabulous. I want a contrast with mine, which will be super-fancy, the whole Princess Diana fantasy thing. I want real roses sewn all over it. Maybe we could get the old gardener to grow them specially. That would be so authentic!'

'How will you keep them fresh?'

'We'll have a team sewing them on hours before the ceremony. It will be so great. I'll be like a walking, talking English rose garden. Is there a rose garden for the photos? Never mind, we'll build one.'

Molly glanced nervously at Mama, but there was still no movement in her expression. Was she being discreet about her feelings? Or had she recently refreshed her fillers?

'Lord Byron marries Jane Austen.' Molly mulled the image over in her mind. 'That is a great concept, mixing the classic, dashing, romantic, poetic hero with early Me-Too. Great.'

Zahara stared at her for a few silent moments, processing the thoughts. 'Wow,' she said eventually. 'That's a great concept statement. I love it. I need to see the house. We can go now.'

'I don't know if—'

'I'll get them to bring the car.' Mama cut Molly's protest off.

'We should buy the old guy a new puppy on the way!' Zahara clapped her hands like an excited child. 'I know exactly the place to go.'

'Don't worry about the car,' Molly said, 'I can drive us.'

'In a Mini?' Mother and daughter spoke in unison, with identical looks of horror.

'No,' Molly said, 'don't worry. I'm in the Range Rover today.'

As they vacated the kitchen, the staff reappeared from wherever they had been discreetly waiting, off camera, and resumed their daily chores.

CHAPTER SIX

'Would you actually call that a puppy?' Zahara mused, filming from the front passenger seat as her mother struggled with the over-excited Alsatian, who had climbed over from the boot of the Range Rover onto her lap, where it stood, panting, head now wedged between the front seats, apparently eager to get a better view of the road ahead. Mama was clutching the dachshund to her chest, as if to save it from being eaten.

'You could have had one of the cute little ones,' Mama pointed out, 'if you had just been willing to wait a few weeks for them to be old enough to leave their mother.'

'I despise waiting,' Zahara replied, ignoring her mother's exasperated eye-roll. 'Delayed gratification is for the birds. The old man is sad, he needs a distraction from his grief now! And how often do you see a pure white Alsatian? He's like a god, come to Earth in dog form.'

'Looks more like some sort of Arctic wolf to me,' Molly said as Zahara stopped filming. 'The original wolf in sheep's clothing. You were lucky that woman was a fan. I don't think many decent breeders would let you just waltz off with a puppy at the first meeting.'

'She liked being filmed,' Zahara said. 'Everyone wants their fifteen minutes of fame. Plus, she knows me and I paid way more than she was asking.'

'What if the old man doesn't want another dog yet?' Mama interjected from the back. 'Suppose he wants to have a period of mourning for his old one?'

'Then we'll keep him. I love him already.'

'I'm not picking up his poop,' Mama said. 'Just so you know.'

Zahara pretended not to hear as she turned back and opened the vanity mirror on the car's sun visor to check on her own perfection. 'What have you told them about me?'

'Told who?' Molly asked.

'The old people in the house.'

'Nothing,' Molly said, laughing. 'Your secrets are all safe with me. What do you want me to tell them?'

'I don't have secrets. I'm an open book. Millions of people know every detail of my life. Do they realise what an opportunity this is for them to make their venue go viral?'

'I don't think they even watch television, let alone social media. A virus would mean something very different to them.'

'My God.' Zahara applied another layer of gloss to her famously luscious lips, pouting like she was bursting open a ripe, exotic fruit, and snapped the sun visor back up. 'That's incredible. I love it. I doubt Jane Austen or Lord Byron would have been online much, if it had been around in their day. They would have had no time for waiting around in hideous television studios to be cross-examined by some nobody, either. Too busy writing novels and poetry and going to exquisitely elegant balls, and having wonderful love affairs. Life was so great for celebrities back then.'

Mama made a derisory clucking sound with her tongue, which the puppy mistook for an invitation to wipe her immaculately painted face with a saliva-drenched tongue, gaining purchase with his front paws on her gold-covered cleavage.

'I really think we should have warned them we are coming,' Molly said, not for the first time since they set out on their mission.

'No. I want it to be a fabulous surprise, with the puppy and everything. I can't wait to see their reactions. They have to be authentically surprised for it to work.'

Mama repeated the clucking sound and surprised the puppy with a punch as it lunged in for another taste.

'Mama!' Zahara admonished her.

'What?' Mama pretended to be puzzled.

'You can't do that! Your rings will hurt him!'

'I can't do what? I can't protect myself? Would you tell me I can't protect myself from a rapist in the street?'

The puppy, appearing to mistake the punch for a new game, smothered the rest of her reply by climbing onto her lap and filling her mouth with a furry ear, as the dachshund struggled, goggle-eyed, to clamber up from underneath and reach oxygen. Molly concentrated on her driving and tried not to imagine the scene that lay ahead.

• • •

'You again?' Mrs Woodcock said, as she opened the door to Molly's knock. 'What do you want?'

'My client—' Molly waved in the direction of the car '—would really like to see round the house. She's with her mother. The mother of the bride.'

'Now?' Mrs Woodcock couldn't disguise her irritation. 'I've just made myself a cup of tea. I've been up since five.'

'I'm happy to take them round myself,' Molly assured her. 'If that's all right with you. We won't disturb you. We should have called first, I know, but my client is so eager to see the place …'

'Why?'

'I showed her the film I shot when I was here last time. She loved what she saw. She is a very spontaneous person.'

'No dogs inside,' Mrs Woodcock warned, spotting the puppy, which was still standing on Mama's lap, but was now also licking the car window in its eagerness to escape.

'The dog is a gift, actually,' Molly admitted sheepishly.

'For whom?'

'Benson. To replace the one he lost.'

Mrs Woodcock, lost for words, turned on her heel and headed back to the kitchen and to her waiting cup of tea, leaving the open front door as a reluctant invitation.

Mama, tired of being made to wait, opened the car door and the puppy flowed out in a joyous avalanche of white fur, pink tongue and thrashing tail, galloping into the house and skidding across the parquet before Mama had even struggled to her feet and adjusted her clothing and lap dog.

'She likes us to take our shoes off,' Molly said, as Mama reached the French doors.

'Who does?' Mama's immaculately shaped eyebrows arched threateningly. 'The housekeeper?'

There was enough information in the way she drawled out Mrs Woodcock's title for Molly to know that it was not worth repeating herself. She unlaced her own Doc Martens, struggling to keep the puppy from knocking her over as she crouched.

'I … Just … Love … It!' Zahara squealed as she swung her camera around and up the grand staircase, settling on the regal painting of the Colonel and his wife. 'Look at these people! It is so English. It is so Jane Austen. It is so Mr Darcy.'

'Everything is so old,' Mama muttered. 'It must be so dirty.'

She ran one tiny, beringed finger along a surface, obviously surprised by how pristinely clean it proved to be on close inspection. She pulled her glasses down from the top of her head for an even closer look, but found nothing to complain about. She tutted anyway.

'Let's go find the old gardener guy,' Zahara said, dancing in excited circles as the puppy clawed enthusiastically at her, its head almost up to her chin, its long tongue lashing out for a taste of the perfume that smelled irresistibly delicious on her smooth throat. Because she was still filming, she lacked the ability to defend herself and did not want her fans to hear her losing her temper with an innocent, besotted puppy. 'I can't wait to see his face when we show him what we've got for him.'

Mrs Woodcock was also watching Benson's face as she stood by the kitchen window with her cup and saucer. He was outside the kitchen door, hacking at an ancient apple tree with the panga his father had brought back after doing his time in the army in Kenya, when the puppy careened around the corner, tongue flapping happily in the wind. The blade glinted in what was left of the evening's sunlight as he instinctively raised it to protect himself from attack.

'Mr Benson!' Molly shouted, her voice almost drowned by the shrieks of her clients. 'It's me, Molly, from the pub!'

Mrs Woodcock realised she had been holding her breath for several seconds, and exhaled a sigh of resignation as Molly caught the jumping, twisting puppy by the scruff of its neck, and clung on like a rider in a rodeo, as she explained to Benson that it was an unasked-for gift. The old gardener's face remained as unmoved as granite, and the raised panga remained poised to strike.

'It's for you,' Mama shouted. 'For God's sake. The dog is for you, man.'

Zahara continued to film and laughed merrily. 'OMG! He is so surprised. It's going to take him a bit of time to process this. This is sooo cute! What a great moment. Can we take a tour of the gardens? They are sooo beautiful! Sooo wild! This place must have been sooo wonderful when it was all new!'

• • •

Mrs Woodcock took another sip of tea as she watched the scene unfold. She remembered the puppies that were born to the gun dogs, when she was a child, that she and Benson had only ever been allowed to play with in the stables, under adult supervision. He wasn't 'Benson' then, just 'Little Tom'. His father had not yet relinquished the title. She was still Phyllis, or 'Fine Little Filly' as the old Colonel would joke every time that he came across her in the house, clinging nervously to her mother's skirts.

'Can we take them inside to play?' the children had begged as the puppies squirmed in their arms, crawling up to lick their faces and nipping at their fingers with needle-like teeth, but old Benson never allowed it.

'They're working dogs, they are,' he would tell them. 'You can't go mollycoddling them like they were your pets. The Colonel would have my guts for garters.'

The children understood the concept of working dogs, and they never felt the urge to cuddle the fox hounds that lived behind the bars of their prison-like enclosure in the stables' courtyard. Sometimes they would watch in awe as the hounds tore into the raw meat that old Benson, or one of the other hunt servants, threw in to them, and both of them had been knocked off their feet by the pack at one time or another. She still felt a guilty thrill when she remembered how exciting it had been for her and Little Tom to watch the hunt meeting outside the house and sweeping away down the drive and through the village, forcing cars to stop and people to hurriedly close their gates to keep the foaming tide of hounds from trashing their front gardens in their mind-less search for a scent. The power and noise of the men and women on their high horses, with their big voices and red faces, was both intimidating and intoxicating. Every time she pictured it, she would hear Bryan's gentle voice whispering inside her head, telling them both how cruel the hunt was, and how he would ban it once the estate was his. He looked so sad when he talked about how brutally the hounds tore the foxes they caught to pieces that she couldn't help but share his pain. But still the sight of them, and the sounds of the horses' hooves clattering on the tarmac, the hunting horns blaring out their rallying cries, the shouts of the hunts-men, and the hounds baying for blood, had always made her guilty heart beat a little faster.

Sometimes, if old Mr Benson and the Colonel were not around, Bryan would sneak out to the stables with her and Little Tom to see a new litter of gun dogs. He wasn't like the other grown-ups. He treated both the children and the animals like they were much-loved pets. He could recognise each of the puppies by the names that he had invented for them, or borrowed from whatever book he was reading at the time. It was easy with the spaniels, because of their differ-ent markings, but the labs were nearly all a uniform black, not yet old enough to have developed distinguishing features.

'How do you know which is which?' she remembered asking him.

He'd laughed, his smile so handsome she could hardly bear the pain of looking at him, but couldn't tear her wide eyes away. 'I have no idea, Phil. Maybe I'm just imag-ining I can.'

She liked to believe that he wasn't imagining it, that he could see the souls inside each of the soft, squirming little pouches of life. As a child she liked to think about Bryan whenever she could; even now she still found a comforting sadness in remembering how he was before he grew old, and before his body became weak and threadbare. She remembered how she used to make Little Tom hide in the bushes with her, so they could watch Bryan and his friends around the swimming pool, when the Colonel was away in London, or shooting in Scotland. That was before those friends gradually deserted him. She could get Little Tom to do whatever she wanted in those days, before he started to develop a mind of his own. It was hard to imagine what a sweet-natured little boy he was, now that he had been such a cussed old man for so long.

She had to confess, if only to herself, that even as a small child she had experienced the first pinprick of jealousy whenever she saw one of Bryan's flamboyant friends stealing a chance to squeeze his bare, brown shoulder, tousle his wet hair, wrestle with him in the water, or peck him on the cheek. They all seemed so happy and carefree to be around him, even after everything they had been through by then, none of which she knew anything about at the time, all vying for his attention and his approval. They had all tried so hard to recreate the carefree times of the past, although by then it was already too late and it wouldn't be long before the last of them gave up trying. The original good times, which had taken place when Philly and Little Tom were still babies, had been too badly trampled on to ever be resurrected or sustained for more than the occasional drunken afternoon. They could only be imitated, in short bursts of forced high spirits, aided by copious jugs of Pimm's, and other substances, which she also knew nothing about at the time. She hated that these friends could still make him laugh so much more easily than she could, jolting him out of the introspective state he inhabited most of the time, even if it was only for a few hours at a time. He was still the centre of all their worlds, just as he was the centre of hers, and that seemed like the natural place for him to be. She came to despise them all for abandoning him the way they eventually did, but still she was glad when the cars stopped rolling up the drive on sunny afternoons, and she and Little Tom had him to themselves, with no one older or cleverer, or funnier, arriving to seduce him away from them.

He taught them both how to swim, after she nagged and begged for a whole summer, and she could still make herself shiver by conjuring up the sensation of his long fingers supporting her as she paddled frantically to stay afloat, and the excitement of clambering onto his shiny, wet, slippery shoulders and jumping into the water, once she had learned how to bob back to the surface, laughing and spluttering with joy. Afterwards, once Bryan had disappeared up to his bedroom to change, her mother would take her and Little Tom into the kitchen, wrap them in towels and sit them in front of the Aga to dry. If she thought about it hard enough, she would have to admit that it had probably only happened on a few occasions, but those occasions were amongst the most vivid and cherished images from a seventy-year collection of memories.

Before they became distant memories, they provided her with the raw material for her girlhood fantasies. At night, when she was alone in her bedroom, and she could hear the murmur of her parents' voices safely downstairs, she would turn her eiderdown into a wedding dress, and imagine herself walking down the aisle towards the altar and towards a waiting, smiling Bryan. Everyone would be jealous of her when he gently lifted her veil and kissed her, because they would be able to see that she was in heaven. She was sure his lips would taste like the strawberries that Old Benson grew in the walled garden, and which he allowed her and Little Tom to sample in exchange for their picking services. Sometimes she and Little Tom would also be able to retrieve them from the empty Pimm's glasses once pool parties were over and her mother was clearing up the careless mess that the visitors left behind them, wherever they went.

• • •

Benson had lowered the panga and was crouching down to pat the puppy, which had rolled subserviently onto its back to receive the attention, as Zahara continued to film the encounter. Mrs Woodcock drained her teacup to drown out the twitch of anger she felt deep in her soul at the sight of Benson receiving so much attention and kindness from strangers. It stirred a thousand bitter memories.

CHAPTER SEVEN

'Oh look. They gave the old boy a puppy! That is so cute!'

'Who gave who a puppy?'

Several more drinkers leaned in to look over Betty's shoulder at her phone.

'What sort of dog is that?'

'Must be an albino.'

'Never seen that before. Looks like a ghost dog.'

'What happened to the old dog he had with him that night he came in here?'

'He shot it,' Joan announced from behind the bar, pleased to be ahead of the internet with the news.

'He shot it?'

'He still has a gun? Didn't the police confiscate it?'

'He's a gamekeeper. He's bound to have a gun. They can't take away a man's living.'

More people moved across the room to watch the screen as Betty repeated the video of Benson becoming acquainted with the puppy as it leapt up, almost toppling him in its eagerness to be loved.

'Looks like he's about to chop its head off!'

'Oh, that's adorable. What's he calling it?'

'Bryan, apparently,' Joan informed the room, without looking up from the pint she was pulling.

'After the dead man?'

Joan shrugged, placing the filled glass on the bar and starting another. She only knew as much as Molly had told her in a hurried phone call from her car as she sped back to Peckham after dropping Zahara and her mother home the previous evening.

'That's a bit weird.'

'Who gave him this puppy?' a latecomer to the story enquired.

'This woman that Molly works for.'

'Her name is Zahara. She's an influencer.' Betty obviously found it extraordinary that the older pub denizens were not familiar with someone who was such a permanent fixture in her own online life and imagination. 'And quite possibly the most beautiful woman ever!'

'She's a rich bitch!' her boyfriend muttered. 'Her dad owns like a thousand hotels around the world.'

'All right, Mr Grumpy!' Betty elbowed him in the ribs and replayed the video once more for the latecomers to the crowd now surrounding her.

'It's going to be a job to keep a dog like that clean in the winter,' someone observed.

'The old boy didn't seem that good at keeping himself clean, never mind a dog ...'

'But what does she do exactly? This Zahara?' someone else from the back asked.

'She's an influencer,' Betty repeated slowly, as if she was

talking to the children in the nursery where she worked three mornings a week. 'She lives this great life, and she's really funny.'

'It's easy to live a great life if your daddy is a billionaire,' her boyfriend pointed out again.

'She makes her own money.' Betty was becoming defensive to the point of angry. 'She's got, like, millions of followers.'

'He shot that poor old dog?' Someone who had not troubled to leave their stool at the bar had obviously been considering the earlier news item. 'The one that came in here the other night and snored under the bar?'

'It was a mercy killing. The poor thing could hardly walk.'

'And it never stopped farting.'

'There's a few people around here who could do with shooting,' Joan said, holding out the card machine for the round-payer to tap.

'Like poor old Bryan in the big house?' someone said, eliciting a few knowing sniggers.

Joan stared at the card machine, waiting for it to connect, and pretended not to hear. Daisy quietly left her table in the darkest corner of the room, and disappeared upstairs to her bedroom.

'Who's she marrying, then?' the conversation round the phone screen continued. 'This client of your Molly's?'

'A footballer.'

'Which footballer?'

'Her.' Betty held up a picture of Carolyn and there was a moment or two of quiet as everyone adjusted their preconceived ideas.

'Nice looking,' someone ventured cautiously.

'She's gorgeous,' Betty agreed, as if challenging the room to disagree, 'they both are. They make the most beautiful couple.'

Her boyfriend opened his mouth, but reconsidered whatever thought he had been about to release into the conversation.

. . .

The following morning, Zahara put in an excited call to her father in Dubai. His personal assistant diverted her to his personal lawyer, Charu, which cooled Zahara's enthusiasm immediately. Charu assured her, with well-trained kindness, that there was no chance of her being able to speak to her father that day, but that she would be pleased to pass on a message. Zahara told her about the house and how much she wanted to be married there.

'Let me do some research,' Charu said once she had taken the details, 'and I will see if I can persuade him for you.'

Zahara was about to protest that she would prefer to do the persuading of her father personally, but Charu had already hung up. Mama was listening from the other side of the room, her face even more of an impenetrable, frozen mask than usual. Not a single muscle was moving. She didn't even move her tongue in order to tut.

. . .

A few days later, Daisy woke up to the smell of smoke, when normally she could only smell the deposits that the early morning horses left on the high street, below her bedroom window. There were no alarms to be heard, and no panicked voices, so she assumed she was not in any immediate danger. Pulling back the curtains, she found the view she had enjoyed every other day of her stay was entirely obscured. This was not the sort of mist that occasionally occurred as a cold night prepared to become a warm day, but it did explain the smell, which she soon discovered had infiltrated deep into every corner of the pub, overcoming the usual musky aromas of beer and dust.

'It is very smoky out there,' she mentioned to Joan as she came into the bar for breakfast.

'It's coming from the big house,' Joan informed her. 'I believe they've started to clear the undergrowth.'

'So, they have started already to prepare for the wedding, so soon?'

'Apparently the bride loves the place, and wants to be married there next summer. It seems to be happening surprisingly fast.'

'Your daughter must be very pleased to have such a happy client.'

'Yes.' Joan was surprised that Daisy had been following what had been going on around her that closely. 'I think she is.'

'It will be nice for you too,' Daisy ventured, 'to have her working in the village?'

Joan paused for a second, as if this was an angle she hadn't considered before. 'Yes,' she said. 'It is nice. I do miss having her around.'

'But London is not too far, no?'

'Not as the crow flies,' Joan agreed, 'but when you are running a pub, you can't just close up and go off at the drop of a hat, so she might as well have moved to the other side of the world. She needed to get away from the village. There was nothing here for her.'

'But now there is.'

'So it seems.'

'We all get pulled back to our roots eventually, don't you find?'

'I never really went anywhere. I've been rooted here all my life.'

'You are lucky.'

'Maybe. I would have liked to see a bit of the world, but it's too late now.'

Daisy gave a Gallic shrug. 'You have everything that is needed for a good life here. Being a tourist all your life, never staying anywhere long enough to put down roots, is not so great.'

• • •

Two hours later, with Trotsky for company, Daisy was skirting the walls of the estate once more, upwind of the mountainous bonfires that had now been coating the village in smoke for several hours. Gangs of young men were at work with machetes, chainsaws and axes, circled by other, better dressed young men, holding film cameras, and girls with clipboards, headphones and takeaway coffees.

'Bryan!' The angry shout from the other side of the wall made her turn, just in time to see the Alsatian coming up over the stones with Trotsky in his sights. Taken by surprise by the unexpected apparition, Daisy failed to tighten her grip on the lead and the two dogs raced away down the track together, both apparently filled with joy at the prospect of sharing an adventure, Trotsky's lead bouncing along behind his scuttling back legs. Benson clambered over the wall, with considerably more difficulty than the puppy, and stood beside Daisy as they watched the dogs disappear over the horizon.

'They'll be back,' he said, after a few moments' reflection. 'They always come back.'

'I hope so,' Daisy said. 'It's not my dog. I'm just walking it.'

'He's still a puppy,' Benson said, 'the Alsatian. He's trainable. They use them as police dogs, don't they?'

'Yes, I'm sure.'

Daisy was surprised to find herself unable to think of anything else to say. Benson was aware that she was staring at him hard, before averting her eyes quickly, as if embarrassed to have been caught.

'They're making a documentary,' Benson said eventually, breaking the silence that had fallen between them as they stood together, watching the men at work.

'A documentary about what?'

Benson shrugged. 'Some fancy wedding and all the preparations.'

'A sort of wedding-property-makeover show?' Daisy smiled sympathetically.

Benson looked at her blankly. 'They're making a right

mess of the grounds, is all I can say. But they have plenty of money to put it right. More money than sense, some might say. The trouble with common sense is that it's not so common these days.'

'But maybe it is an answer to your problems?' Daisy suggested. 'Better than a caravan site.'

'Better than a caravan site,' he agreed with what sounded a little like a chuckle, relighting the ragged cigarette attached to his dry lower lip, as if settling in for a long conversation. 'See that willow?' He nodded towards a tree that soared about fifty feet into the sky above them, weeping down in waterfalls of branches. 'Planted that as a sapling.'

'My goodness.' Daisy was genuinely impressed. 'That must be very satisfying for you. They're not touching that, are they?'

'Over my dead body. It's got a preservation order. Don't trust them though. I'm watching every move. None of them know anything about trees. They're just hired hands. Foreigners.' Daisy thought she spotted a glint of mischief in the old man's eyes. 'Eastern Europe,' he added, as if to reassure her that she was not a foreigner, at least not as much of one as they were. She nodded her understanding and her appreciation of what was obviously intended to be a compliment.

'Are they working inside the house as well?' she asked.

'They're going in and out, making a lot of noise. Don't know what they're doing. I'm not allowed in the house, not without an invitation from Her Majesty.'

'Mrs Woodcock?'

'Phyllis.' He nodded.

'She's the boss?'

'Thinks she is. Been like that ever since she was born.'

'You must be very close,' Daisy said, 'being here together all your lives. That must be very nice. I moved many times, all through my life. Now my mother has died, there is no one who has known me from the beginning.'

Benson gave no sign of having heard her as he took a long drag on his butt-end before setting off after the dogs.

• • •

At that moment, Mrs Woodcock was mopping up the footprints that the army of plumbers and builders had left across the parquet in the hall on their way to the main staircase, which was safely covered in plastic. She was going to have to find some sheets to cover the floor. The project manager had informed her that the workers had been pulled off a refurbishment job at a hundred-room hotel in Birmingham, and would be in the house for several weeks, installing the required en-suite bathrooms to all the bedrooms. Hardly any of them seemed to speak English, so there was no point in her trying to persuade them to remove their boots.

'The boss's daughter is getting married,' he said, 'and she's talked Daddy into putting us on the job. Apparently, it's a priority.'

'Don't they need planning permission?' she asked. 'For a historic house like this?'

The manager shrugged. 'Not my problem, love. If the boss says it's all been okayed, that is all I need to know. He's got more lawyers than you and me have had hot dinners. Plus, he knows people in government. Got them in his pocket, so to speak …' He tapped the side of his nose conspiratorially, and allowed that thought to hang in the air.

'All right for some,' Mrs Woodcock said, trying to take in the disquieting idea that so much could be achieved so quickly when nothing in her life had changed for so long. It had been many years since such a torrent of money had flowed through the house. Witnessing it roar back with such force was awakening emotions that she was unfamiliar with. She could feel control of the minutiae of her life slipping away as surely as it had evaded her when she was a child, when Bryan's father was still in charge and everyone had to bend to his will, walking on eggshells whenever he was around. She noticed that a cameraman had come in from outside and was recording their conversation. 'Boots off when you come inside,' she snapped, before returning to her polishing, uncomfortably conscious that the camera was still trained on her and still running. The man had not taken his boots off, although she was certain that he had heard her.

• • •

Outside, Trotsky's lead had snagged on the spikes of a low hawthorn branch, tethering him to an overgrown hedge as Bryan danced around him and he barked back with mock ferocity, allowing Benson and Daisy to catch up. Daisy pulled her scarf up over her mouth and nose to keep out the sting of the smoke from the bonfires and Benson drew so deeply on his roll-up it glowed a fierce orange as he looped a noose-style length of rope around Bryan's neck. He pulled it tight, making the puppy twist in the air and choke as he continued to leap around his new playmate, like a rebellious child refusing to come in for its tea. With no visible sign of anger, Benson ripped a whip-like branch from the hedge and beat the Alsatian repeatedly, until it whimpered to a halt at his feet, gazing up at him with wide, imploring eyes and a lolling tongue. Daisy winced, but held her tongue. On the far side of the field, a motionless fox watched the scene unfolding, poised to trot away if necessary.

CHAPTER EIGHT

'Carolyn.' Zahara's Mama took a firm grip of her future daughter-in-law's arm and led her towards the walled garden, while Zahara was distracted by the lighting designer, who wanted to explain how he was going to illuminate the exterior of the house, projecting pictures from the happy couple's social media sites onto the pillars and walls in an ever-swirling kaleidoscope of happy memories. 'I need to talk to you.'

Carolyn was well used to receiving 'talks' from Mama and, over the months, she had grown skilful at deflecting the older woman's attempts at manipulation. She could understand that Mama was having to make a great many adjustments to her expectations for her daughter and believed that she deserved to be listened to. She also knew that if Zahara knew half of what her mother was saying when she was not within earshot, she would be furious. Carolyn was anxious not to cause any more rifts in the family when they all had so many other things to be thinking about, so she listened to both of them when they let off steam to her, smiled and nodded, or put on a concerned expression if that seemed appropriate, and tried to say as little as possible, conserving any aggression that might dwell in her soul for the football pitch. She really didn't feel there was much more she could contribute against two such primal forces of nature anyway.

'You need to talk to her,' Mama said as she steered Carolyn to one of the moss-covered stone benches that overlooked the raised beds. 'You are the only one she will listen to. You, she respects.'

'Oh no, Mama,' Carolyn insisted, although she liked to think that might be true, 'that is not true. She respects you totally. She just enjoys teasing you. You have such a good relationship. You have such a wonderful sense of humour.' She could feel the eyes of Mama's dog fixed on her face from his position in Mama's lap, and forced herself not to glance down, for fear of feeling judged for her insincerity.

Mama seemed not to have heard her as she ploughed on along her pre-prepared furrow of thought. 'This place is not suitable. However many rainforest showers Vijay puts in, however many trees we fill with twinkly-twinkly lights, however many marquees we build. It just isn't big enough. There were over a thousand people at my wedding to Vijay, maybe two thousand. I don't remember exactly. There were elephants! How is that possible in this little place? Where will everyone stay? This place will not do. We need a more suitable venue. Somewhere with many good hotels and shopping malls for people to amuse themselves. You have to persuade her to listen. The guests will be here for days; what will they do if they can't go shopping?'

'I'm sure that you and Zahara will be able to make this place look wonderful.' Carolyn squeezed Mama's dainty, fluttering hand reassuringly. For an unsettling moment it reminded her of Zahara's, until the cold, wet nose of the dachshund intervened. 'And there is going to be a lot of entertainment. She has set her heart on the place, and she has Molly to help her …'

'Molly is a lovely girl,' Mama agreed, unconvincingly, 'but she has no experience of the sort of wedding a family like ours should put on.'

'Zahara trusts her completely. We both do. Zahara is on top of every detail.'

'Everyone will know that we are paying, because …' Mama fluttered her hands again, as if searching for the right words, '… because there is not a groom. It will reflect badly on Vijay if the venue is not suitable. People will think he has been stingy. He will be inviting many important people. They will see and they will judge him. They might decide he is not such a good person to do business with.'

'Times are very different from when you and Vijay were married,' Carolyn said, pretending not to have heard the comment about the absence of a groom. She wondered if Mama was asking her to contribute financially. She didn't mind, in theory, but wasn't sure that anything she was able to afford would make much of a difference to the ocean of expense rising around them. She decided not to open that particular can of worms. 'What does Vijay think?'

'Zahara has her father round her little finger. Anything she wants, he will say yes. I have tried to reason with him. He tells me, "Don't worry, Mama, I will see to everything", but how can one man see to everything in the world? He says he has already spoken to ministers in the British government about planning regulations. He takes on so much. He will give himself a heart attack. I worry, Carolyn. The worry will be the death of me.'

'He seems to have committed a lot of people and money to the restoration already. He must feel confident it is the right place.'

'He has not even seen it!' Mama wailed. 'I tell him he is wasting money here. I tell him he is pouring money down the drain. These old people are taking us for a ride. They are laughing at us. He is making their house beautiful again for them and they are so rude to us. He says I shouldn't worry because his lawyers are taking care of everything.' Mama sounded like she was having to work hard to hold back tears of exasperation. 'He tells me it will be a good investment, although I can't see how. He says he will be inviting the prime minister to the wedding. He has all these people to keep happy. It is too much for one man. I will be a widow if he carries on like this.'

'Have you asked the lawyers what they think?' Carolyn asked.

'I don't have anything to do with Vijay's business arrangements,' she snapped, and Carolyn remembered something Zahara had told her one tearful night, about her father and his personal lawyer.

'Zahara knows what she is doing,' she said, eager to calm Mama's rising level of distress. 'She has inherited your great taste. Let's just trust her.'

'I can see you are determined not to help me.' Mama ended the conversation, standing up, hoisting the dog under her arm and vigorously brushing the moss from her sari. 'She has you under her spell, Carolyn, just like her father. You must stand up to her. You must put your foot down. She is too wilful for her own good. She always was.'

'I know, Mama, it is one of the reasons I love her so much.'

Mama swept regally through the gate in the wall, pushing past a cameraman who had sensed a drama in the air and was hoping to capture it for the enjoyment of future viewers. Carolyn sat for a few moments, aware that even though Mama had gone, the cameraman was still filming her, sitting alone on the bench, and that there was nothing to gain from protesting that he was invading her privacy. If she wasn't careful, she would look like Princess Diana when she was photographed sitting tragically alone in front of the Taj Mahal. Zahara's media circus was in full swing, there was no point hoping for even a few moments of privacy in which to gather her thoughts while living in her orbit. If she said anything unguarded it would be recorded and might well appear in the documentary, influencing the way she would be depicted in the media for months or even years to come. She had only been in a relationship with Zahara for six months, but she was already more skilled at handling her image, and the narrative that the public were building around her, than she had been when she was just a moderately famous footballer. At least this time Mama hadn't tried to talk her into standing aside for the man she and her husband had originally chosen for Zahara, which was a first, so that was a step forward, of sorts.

She knew that when Mama was talking with Vijay in private, she blamed him for introducing her to their daughter. Their first meeting had happened at a press reception, held to announce that Vijay was buying Carolyn's team. Zahara had been filming the occasion, of course, and had obviously wanted her followers to meet the star player. The attraction was instant, mutual and overwhelming. By the end of the interview, during which neither of them could stop staring at the other, both of them were well on their way to being in love.

'If you had not put them together that evening,' she had overheard Mama telling her husband over WhatsApp, on more than one occasion, 'none of this nonsense would have happened, and maybe I would be looking forward to receiving some grandchildren.'

Vijay had tried talking his daughter out of the relationship at the beginning, during a family weekend at the Villa d'Este on Lake Como, but she had just laughed at him, kissed him on the forehead and made him feel foolish and out of touch with the modern world. That stung because he prided himself on having his finger on the world's pulse, and he did not have the time to turn the issue into a full-scale war, even if he had wanted to. As long as his little girl was happy, he could tolerate his own personal discomfort at this break with tradition. He liked to boast in interviews that he was a 'disruptor' in the business world, so he could hardly complain at the disruption his daughter was now provoking in their wider family. If only he could persuade her mother to accept it too, his life would be a great deal more peaceful.

Carolyn took a deep breath and stood up, smiled disarmingly into the unresponsive eye of the camera, and tossed her long blonde hair in a way that she had learned would reflect the sunlight well, as she strode through the gate towards the house. She eventually found Zahara in one of the bedrooms, having finished with the lighting designer, curled up amongst the pillows on an intricately carved four-poster bed, as the plumbers and builders worked around her, moderating their language out of respect for the boss's daughter, who was talking to her camera. As always, Carolyn couldn't help but smile at the sight of her beauty and the joyful sound of her enthusiasm.

'Hi, Caro!' Zahara patted the faded eiderdown beside her, welcoming her onto the bed and into the frame of the picture. 'Look at these fabulous photographs I've found.'

Zahara slid a mould-speckled photograph album across and repositioned herself so that her viewers could see Carolyn carefully turning the pages and lifting the fragile leaves of parchment that covered each black and white photograph.

'Aren't they fabulous? Like works of art, but with real people from the past. It's living history.'

To Carolyn they looked like a bunch of effete young men posing as statues in outlandish costumes. Some of them were wearing headdresses that looked as if they had made them themselves from peacock feathers and flowers, fruit and anything else they could find. Some of them were in short togas, showing off shapely calves and thighs. It was almost drag, but not quite, more like mock-historical tableaux, re-enacted by a local amateur dramatics' society, given a tinge of artistic merit by the faded monochrome of the photography. She murmured something appreciative for Zahara's benefit, and for however many fans might be sharing the experience.

'Look at the backgrounds,' Zahara urged her, sensing that Carolyn was not fully appreciating what she was being shown, 'they must all have been taken here, around the house and the grounds. You can see how fabulous the place must have looked back then.'

'It all looks very exotic,' Carolyn agreed, a little doubtfully. 'Where did you find them?'

'The album was hidden under the pillows here. This was the old man's bed. He must have kept them there so that he could look at them when he was alone and feeling a bit low. Taking a stroll down memory lane, reliving a time when he was young and beautiful and carefree. Don't you think that is just adorable? I'm trying to work out which one is him. Doesn't the house look fabulous?'

'This is the bed he died in?' Carolyn looked around her at the aged bedclothes and lightly discoloured pillow.

'Oh.' Zahara had obviously not considered that possibility. 'I don't know. Maybe. Gross!' She wrinkled her nose prettily, but Carolyn resisted the temptation to kiss her in front of the camera. 'But look at the pictures. Some of them have names written on the back. We need to google all of them. I bet they are all like lords and dukes and earls and stuff. Maybe even royalty!'

Carolyn laughed. She loved the permanent whirl of excitement that Zahara existed in, a strangely childlike state of joy and wonder, despite the obvious sophistication of her family upbringing. Her high spirits were infectious, impossible to resist, whatever mood you might be in yourself. At least, that was how they touched her, and she assumed that the millions of people who chose to follow Zahara online felt something similar.

'We should try to reproduce some of these scenes for the wedding.' Zahara was still talking as Carolyn kept turning the pages for the benefit of the camera, barely concentrating on what she was seeing as she basked in the warmth of her lover's aura. 'We could find actors who look like the original people. It would be like turning the clock back. With music from the time playing in the background. Who would that be, do you think? Bing Crosby? Glenn Miller? Frank Sinatra? Ella Fitzgerald? Nina Simone? Noel Coward? Nat King Cole? I'll talk to Molly. She can research it.'

'Can't wait to hear you selling that idea to Mama.'

Zahara laughed. 'Mama loves the old music.'

'I can hear you talking about me.' Mama's voice in the doorway was drowned out by the sudden eruption of a power drill starting up in the next bedroom. Zahara pulled a face to the camera, theatrically covering her ears with her hands, before leaning over and pressing the 'off' button.

•　•　•

That evening, Molly had the same photograph album open on a table in the pub, gently turning the pages for the benefit of the audience of drinkers gathered around her.

'So, this is Bryan, the guy who just died?' someone asked.

'Apparently,' Molly said, 'with a bunch of his school friends, or maybe university.'

'Are they putting on plays at the house?'

'Looks like it.'

'These pictures would be seventy years old then.'

'Maybe a bit more.'

'What does your client want you to do with them?'

'She wants them blown up to life-size, and then she wants to reproduce them for real, using actors and models to create tableaux around the house.'

'He was very beautiful as a young man, wasn't he, that Bryan.'

'Makes a good-looking woman in that costume.'

'Looks a bit like you, Molly.'

'Flatterer!' Molly laughed, but was unable to resist taking a closer look.

Daisy glanced up from her iPad a few tables away, but none of them noticed, all of them being too absorbed in the album.

'I thought the theme was Jane Austen and Lord Byron, this is more Cecil Beaton and Oscar Wilde.'

'Well, they are in sort of historical costumes, a bit Greek maybe?' Molly suggested.

'More YMCA, I'd say.'

'Who would have guessed this was all going on in the house …'

'Can't imagine the old Colonel was too happy about it all.'

Daisy averted her eyes back to her own screen, but

continued to listen as the conversation rambled back and forth around the bar.

'What about the other names on the backs of the pictures?' someone asked as Joan put another round of drinks onto the table where Molly was holding court.

'Zahara's had me googling them all. They've nearly all got titles and come from big houses around the country.'

Joan cocked her head to one side so that she could read the list of names that Molly was scrolling through on her phone.

'Gerald Remers?' she said.

'Friend of yours, Mum?' Molly laughed.

'That was the old bloke who was here the other night. I remember why his name rang a bell now. He was a lawyer my parents had some dealings with, years back when they were chucked out of the farm. I think he was the family lawyer for the big house. He had something to do with setting up a trust fund for your education when your grandfather died.'

'There was a trust fund?' Molly sounded genuinely shocked. 'I had a trust fund?'

'Only to be used for your education. We couldn't have afforded that design course without it,' Joan said, sounding like she wished she hadn't mentioned it. 'There's nothing left now.'

Several heads turned back to squint at the picture in the hope of being able to see any likeness to the old man in the pin-striped suit that might have lasted for more than seventy years. After a few seconds they all looked back up in time to see the swish of Daisy's skirt and her ankles disappearing up the stairs towards her bedroom.

CHAPTER NINE

Benson stood in the gate to the walled garden and stared, trying to make sense of the scene in front of him. The freshly trained Bryan sat at his feet, dazzled by the wealth of opportunities for new friendships that were spread out before him. None of the men looked up from their digging, or signified that they had seen the old man and his glowingly white dog watching them.

'Excuse me, mate.' A voice from behind them made them both jump. Bryan leapt to his feet and Benson turned to see a man with a tall trolley, stacked with neatly labelled shelves of plants. As the trolley rolled past, he ripped off one of the labels and read it.

'Are they all the same?' he asked the man as he parked the trolley beside one of the newly dug beds.

'Yep. Iceberg roses. A thousand of them.'

'A thousand?' Benson stood back as another trolley was rolled past. 'Bugger me! You won't get a thousand in here.' He gestured around the walled garden.

'Some of them are for planting round the house,' the man said. 'Apparently, there are some ancient rose beds that can be resurrected.'

'The old rose garden?'

The man shrugged. 'I guess so.'

'Bugger me,' Benson muttered again, then made the man jump with a shout, 'Sit!'

Sensing that Benson's attention was elsewhere, Bryan had moved without permission in order to reach a tempting-looking bone, which the closest workman had turned up and chucked to one side.

Benson narrowed his eyes and relit his roll-up, allowing Bryan to keep hold of his trophy. Some of the men had straightened up from their labours and were talking amongst themselves in a language Benson didn't recognise. Several of them had picked up bones and seemed to be comparing notes as they tried to work out what they might once have been part of. Benson felt a need to blow his nose as he remembered the terrible sounds on the day of the slaughter. It was the only time he ever saw his father cry, and the only time he ever heard his mother swear. It was the day he realised how much they hated the old man who ruled their lives with such casual, high-spirited cruelty, and the day he started to wonder why he and his father were so conditioned to obey the orders the old man issued, however much they might disagree with them.

• • •

Inside the house, Mrs Woodcock was staring at Molly with equal levels of disbelief, anger and suspicion.

'It's just an idea that Zahara had,' Molly was saying, her voice a little unsteady from the intensity of the older woman's furious eyes. 'Nothing is set in stone.'

'You want me to dress as a servant?' Mrs Woodcock asked for the third time, as if she was struggling to believe her own words.

'Well, the idea is to make the whole day feel like a ball from a Jane Austen novel. So, it's like a theatrical costume really.'

'You are renting my home, not me. If you want people in costume, hire actors.'

'We are hiring a lot of professionals,' Molly assured her, 'including actors, but Zahara thought you and Benson might enjoy being part of the day. She just wants everyone to have a good time.'

A trace of a smile flickered across the otherwise furious set of Mrs Woodcock's thread-thin lips. 'You've talked to Benson about this idea?'

'Not yet.'

'You should have your cameras running when you do. Although his language might not be suitable for broadcasting.'

Molly remembered the gun lying casually on the wheelbarrow and the pool of blood around Rotter's head, and slid her phone back into her bag. 'It was just an idea,' she muttered. 'It's not a deal breaker. I think Bryan would have loved it.'

'Bryan?' The sudden hardening of Mrs Woodcock's expression suggested that Molly had just uttered something akin to a blasphemy. 'Loved what?'

'Putting on a show.'

'Why do you say that?' The stare had intensified again, the hint of a smile gone once more.

'I saw pictures of him in shows, when he was young.'

'They were boys. It was a stage. He grew out of it. He didn't like drawing attention to himself once he had grown up. They all took too much drink in those days.' She seemed momentarily flustered by her own anger, and by her anxiety to close the conversation down as quickly as possible. 'They drank too much,' she repeated, her voice cracking in her throat. 'Much too much. His so-called friends were a bad influence. Once they had gone there was no more of that kind of silliness.'

Molly opened her mouth to say more, but Mrs Woodcock was already on her way out of the room, not wanting Molly to see her tears.

. . .

That evening, Daisy listened as the locals around her speculated on the tantalising revelation, conveyed into the pub, in badly broken English, by the workers who had ventured in to refresh themselves at lunchtime, that a large number of bones had risen to the surface of the walled garden at the big house.

'Sounds like the whole place is a mass graveyard,' someone suggested.

'Maybe it's a site of historical interest,' another said. 'Like a Roman burial ground or something. Perhaps they should stop digging until the experts have been called in to take a look.'

'Maybe it's a crime scene. Should someone inform the police?'

'Maybe we should all mind our own business,' Joan suggested. 'Molly will let us know if there is anything we should be worried about.'

'Your Molly has a vested interested in this work going ahead,' a brave voice spoke up, 'maybe she isn't the best person to make that call. Maybe she's part of the problem.'

'Are you intending to nurse that drink all night?' Joan asked. 'Or are you planning to buy a round?'

Daisy kept her eyes on her iPad screen, feeling uncomfortable at the sudden tension that had taken over the evening bar room banter. No one expected her to be part of any round-buying, so she felt she could stay safely outside the sudden flurry of controversy. A few people had attempted to start conversations with her, or offered to buy her a drink, at different times since her arrival, but she had allowed a pretend language barrier to make it hard for them to persevere. A few of the older men had even tried to be flirtatious, but she had given them no encouragement. Most of them had forgotten she was there most of the time. Some of them also assumed she didn't speak English well enough to follow the gossip that swirled around her each evening, often made even more impenetrable to outsiders by the local village accent.

'We don't want the police nosing around the village,' someone said. 'If they start making things difficult for these celebrity wedding people now, then this caravan site might end up happening instead.'

'Has anyone seen any evidence of this caravan site? Are we just taking the word of the two old codgers? Maybe they just wanted to scare us into accepting whatever they decided to do up there.'

'They didn't even know what a wedding venue was,' Joan reminded them, 'so it's hardly likely to be a great conspiracy.'

'Maybe that was a bluff.'

'Or a double bluff.'

'You were the one who suggested it, Joanie,' someone pointed out, without giving any indication whether they were joking. 'Did Molly slip you a few quid?'

Joan pretended not to have heard over the clatter of the glasses she was collecting up.

'I've got a mate who works in planning,' a new voice chimed in, 'who says that someone has ridden roughshod over his whole department regarding everything they are doing up at the house. He wanted to organise a site visit to make sure that they had all the right permissions before they went ahead with tearing the place apart, and he was told to back off, that there had been instructions from the top for them to turn a blind eye. From a minister.'

'Typical establishment cover-up,' Betty's boyfriend chipped in. 'They can literally get away with murder if they're rich enough. If they have been burying bodies up there, then someone needs to say something. They could be the new Fred and Rose West.'

'We don't want the village to become famous for being home to serial killers. That wouldn't help your house values.'

'You think I can afford a house on what they pay me?'

A ripple of laughter rolled round the room. As it faded away, Daisy glanced up and noticed that several of the older customers, seemed to have become thoughtful, staring into their drinks, as if the developments at the big house had dredged up long-buried memories and they were now concentrating on not allowing their imaginations to run away with them.

CHAPTER TEN

'We need to clear out the bedrooms at the top of the house,' Molly said, 'so that the builders can get in there next.'

'I haven't been up there,' Zahara admitted, pulling out her phone and turning on the camera. 'Let's go take a look.'

As she followed Molly up the bare boards of the narrow servants' staircase, she gave a running commentary to the camera. 'This is so exciting. If there are ghosts in the house, this is where they will be hanging out. It is so spooky! It smells bad. I bet no one has been up here for, like, years.' As she continued her breathless narration, Zahara used the bright white light from her phone to cast shadows from the beams and twists of the staircase, zooming in dramatically on thick cobwebs, letting out little squeaks of genuine disgust as they climbed higher and higher, into the shuttered gloom, beyond the realm tamed by many years of Mrs Woodcock's polish and mop.

There were several small bedrooms, each lit with a single, fly-splattered light bulb, and each containing a single bed with wire springs and no mattress. Stacked around the beds were at least three generations-worth of stored suitcases, furniture, a moth-eaten stag's head, stuffed birds in cracked glass cases, broken chairs, which someone perhaps thought they would one day repair, and old clothes housed in disintegrating cloth covers.

'We'll need to get Mrs Woodcock to tell us what we can do with all this junk,' Molly said.

'What's that smell?' Zahara wondered.

'Mothballs, maybe,' Molly ventured, 'or old lavender bags perhaps. My gran's cottage in the village smells like this.'

'I bet there are some real treasures hidden in here. They should get Sotheby's up to have a look. Maybe we'll find a long-lost Rembrandt.'

'Maybe.' Molly sounded doubtful.

'It's a real-life treasure hunt.' Zahara was genuinely excited. She was streaming live, so they were now committed to her pretend adventure. Molly started opening suitcases and rummaging through the old clothes, toys and ornaments, with Zahara letting out excited 'wows' and 'OMGs' at every new find, however mundane.

'OMG, look at this!' she exclaimed, opening another door. 'This is amazing!'

Molly peered over her shoulder into an adjoining room, stacked from floor to ceiling with books. These were nothing like the polished, leather-bound tomes that filled the glass cases in the library. These were dog-eared, much loved paperbacks, their covers curling at the corners, their spines cracked and pages loosened by years of avid handling.

'Georgette Heyer!' Zahara had picked one off the top of a stack and was waving it at the camera. 'I love Georgette Heyer. I think I've read everything she ever wrote. And they are all here!' She dropped to her knees to take a closer look at the titles. 'And *The Scarlet Pimpernel*. I loved *The Scarlet Pimpernel*! Have you read these, Molly? They are exactly how I want the wedding to be! Look, look, the Doctor Syn books! So romantic! So great! One lock of his black hair turned pure white the day his beloved wife died! I mean, come on! Who doesn't want to be loved like that?'

'Not sure I could cope with that much pressure!' Molly laughed and returned to the other room, leaving Zahara to trawl through the piles of books, exclaiming joyfully at every new discovery.

'This one's heavy,' Molly called through to her a few minutes later, as she hauled a battered leather case out from under a bed, 'so maybe it's the family jewels.'

'Maybe gold bullion …' Zahara squeaked, forsaking her reading explorations for a new excitement. 'Is it locked?'

'No.' Molly snapped open the rusted catches. 'It looks like someone's press cuttings.' She dug down through the fading newspaper pages, each layer yellower and more brittle than the one above. 'Hundreds of them. Some of these stories are really old. This one is dated nineteen fifty three.'

Zahara zoomed her camera in on the ancient story.

'It's about this place,' Molly said, having read a couple of lines. 'Something about a police raid and multiple arrests.'

'Wow! This is so exciting! Secret scandals from the past.'

Molly lifted a wad of the cuttings out, spreading them on the floor as Zahara continued to film while they tried to make sense of their discovery. 'Who was Sir John Gielgud?'

'Famous old actor, I think.'

Molly held up the front page of a daily newspaper. 'Arrested for indecency, apparently.'

'Here, in the house?'

'No. In a public toilet in London. Different story.'

'Different story but same theme. This one is from here.' Zahara focused the camera on a front page with pictures of the house in its prime, and several young men being escorted to police cars.

'That's Bryan,' Molly said, reading the caption, 'the same as in that album you found in the bed. He must be about twenty when this happened. I think these are all the guys in those fancy-dress party photos.'

'Which one is him? The really good-looking one?'

'Yeah. I think so.'

'Wow, he really is beautiful! We are going to be finding out a lot more here,' Zahara told her followers. 'And getting back to you with the full story asap.'

She switched the phone off and they both fell silent for a few minutes as they flicked through the articles, becoming uncomfortably aware that their excited flippancy at the discovery might have been misplaced. Something darker and more threatening seemed to be clouding the airless, cluttered little room.

'So, it was illegal to be gay in England?' Zahara asked after a few minutes.

'Apparently so.' Molly didn't look up from the article she was reading.

'Who was Jeremy Thorpe?' Zahara asked a few minutes later.

'I think he was a politician who was exposed for some gay scandal thing. Didn't Hugh Grant play him on television?'

'OMG,' Zahara exclaimed as she read further, 'someone shot this man's dog!'

After taking a few moments to try to make sense of that discovery, they returned to separate, silent reading, turning to one article after another, passing them back and forth between them, pointing to particular headlines, trying to find a pattern within all the apparently random stories.

'So, in the eighties they called AIDS the "gay plague"?' Zahara asked.

'It seems so.' Molly glanced up and saw that Zahara was genuinely stunned by the things she was learning. Her famously huge eyes were brimming with sadness, her lips trembling visibly.

'And they actually used to call it "queer bashing"? Going around looking for gay people to beat up? Did you know any of this?'

'I knew a bit,' Molly said, 'but I thought it was all ancient history. Like the trials of Oscar Wilde, and burning witches at the stake, that sort of thing. There's some stuff about Alan Turing here. Didn't they make a movie about him too?'

'All the stories are about men,' Zahara pointed out. 'Nothing about gay women.'

'And here …' Molly pulled another article from the pile in her hand. 'A guy called Lord Montagu.'

'There's a lot we need to google,' Zahara admitted.

'Why do you suppose someone collected all this material?' Molly gestured at the articles now spread out around them on the bare boards. 'Is it some sort of secret fetish?'

'But it's all negative. It's hardly a celebration of gayness, is it?'

'More of a cautionary tale. Dozens of cautionary tales.'

'Do you think all these guys had something to do with this house?'

'Maybe. I mean, there must have been a lot of house parties here, and these all seem like the sort of people who would have been invited to posh houses. Like the photographs in the album.'

'OMG, this is so English. Like cricket and cream teas. I love it!' Zahara clapped her hands, forcing the sadness down with a resurgence of her habitual high spirits. 'It's perfect Jane Austen and Lord Byron stuff.'

'Maybe we should google Lord Byron too,' Molly suggested. 'Just so we know for sure what we are talking about.'

'Do you think he came here for parties too?' Zahara's mouth had fallen open with childlike wonderment at the idea. 'That would be so cool, if he did!'

· · ·

Since it was a Friday, and since she had no arrangements in London for the weekend, Molly decided to spend it at the pub, once Zahara had been swept away from the big house by her driver. Since both her parents were working all evening, her mother behind the bar, her father in the kitchen, she had ensconced herself in the corner of the snug, as she had so often done as a child, preparing to entertain herself for a few hours by googling on her phone. A solitary, elderly neighbour was the only other drinker in the room.

'You're a history professor, aren't you, Denis?'

'Indeed,' the old man confirmed. 'For my sins.'

'What do you know about Lord Byron?'

'Mad, bad and dangerous to know. That was what Lady Caroline Lamb is supposed to have called him.'

'Bit of a dick, then.'

The old man let out a guffaw of genuine pleasure. 'You might very well say that.'

'If he was around now, I guess he would be cancelled.'

'If he was around now, he would probably be in prison. He seduced and raped everyone he fancied: men, women, children, even his own sister. He also ran up enormous debts. Lords could do that sort of thing in those days. They could pretty much do whatever they wanted. Some of them still do, of course.' He let out another guffaw at his own joke.

'Wow!' Molly realised she was starting to sound like Zahara.

'He wrote some reasonable poetry, though.' Denis was getting into his stride. No one in the pub had asked him for an opinion on a historical figure for a long time. 'And times were very different back then.'

Molly laughed. 'That's what they say about the seventies, all those old disc jockeys and TV presenters.'

'Indeed—' the professor looked nostalgic for a moment '—and in a way they too are right.'

'Still dicks though,' Molly said.

'Yes,' he chuckled, 'and there are still plenty of dicks around today, if the newspapers are to be believed.'

'Oh, you can take my word for it, Denis,' Molly said, thinking of all the men who had stared at her, smirked at her or come on to her in her relatively short adult life, and all the evenings she'd wasted going on dumb dates with unsuitable people who had looked good on the internet. 'There are still plenty of them around. Not just in the newspapers.'

Ending the conversation by returning her attention to her phone, Molly sent Zahara a quick message. 'Done a bit of research. Maybe stop talking online about Lord Byron. Seems he was the greatest perv ever – the Jeffrey Epstein of his day! Maybe talk about Carolyn dressing like Mr Darcy instead. Keep to the Jane Austen theme. That way you'll get instant "brand recognition".'

Zahara came back seconds later with a thumbs-up emoji and a laughing face.

CHAPTER ELEVEN

Normally, when she came home to the village, away from the cramped buzz and rattle of city life, Molly had no difficulty sleeping. The quiet safety of her parents' home, and the village for which the pub had been the steady, beating heart for centuries, provided a security that she had once mistaken for boredom. She had left in search of more glamour and excitement as soon as she was old enough for design school, but the village still offered calm and tranquillity when she needed temporary respite from the stimulation she had found in London and the other big cities she'd spent time in. That night, however, she couldn't stop her mind from churning. The contents of the battered old leather suitcase had unsettled her, although she couldn't quite understand why. Perhaps it had been seeing the unfamiliar tears brimming in Zahara's eyes.

'I'm taking Trotsky for a walk,' she shouted through to her parents in the kitchen the next morning, knowing that they would not be offering to accompany her, since they would be opening their doors to the weekend trade in a few hours. She didn't exactly have a plan, at least not one she could share with anyone else. She just felt drawn back down the drive to the big house.

A variety of heavy machinery was parked along the verges of the drive, which was in the process of being lifted, moved and re-laid so that there would be a one-way system for traffic to get in and out of the estate, unimpeded by having to pull over for oncoming cars. The foundations for a surprisingly large car park had been mapped out, and were already dotted with newly planted, mature trees, which divided each parking place and masked the whole development from the windows and terraces of the house, as well as providing a little cover from any drones that might be taking aerial shots of the landscape.

The front door at the top of the steps stood open and builders were coming and going, despite it being a Saturday morning, so she didn't feel it was inappropriate to wander in, having tethered a disappointed Trotsky to the balustrade. She was pretty sure that if she strolled around the house for long enough, she would eventually bump into Mrs Woodcock, as indeed she did.

'Good morning,' Molly said.

Mrs Woodcock looked up from polishing a silver candle-stick at the dining-room table and nodded an unsmiling response. She seemed to have accepted the fact that she could no longer keep people out of the house and off her parquet floors, but still she was determined to keep the dust and dirt at bay as far as she could, and for as long as she could. Her mother had always taught her that if you let your standards slip, even a little bit, things would soon slide out of control, and once you have allowed that to happen it is not long before you have reached a level of disorder from which you can never recover. She had seen it happen in the gardens and greenhouses that Benson had been unable to keep control of. It was a fear of descending into irredeemable chaos that kept her working from the moment she woke up each morning to the moment she slipped back between her invariably well ironed sheets. Having the house full of workmen with their drills and sanders, however, had created a whole new level of dust for her to keep at bay, and she was not at all sure that she was going to be able to do it for much longer. That thought made her both sad and angry.

Determined not to be intimidated by the older woman's silence, Molly complimented her on the beauty of the silverware, which was spread across the table on well-worn dust-sheets. The housekeeper nodded again, without breaking the rhythm of her muscular arms as they continued to work their magic.

'Would you mind if I asked a question?' Molly ventured. Mrs Woodcock glanced up, but still said nothing. 'Zahara and I were up on the top floor yesterday …'

'I know.'

'There is a suitcase up there, full of newspaper cuttings …'

This time Mrs Woodcock didn't even look up, but it seemed to Molly that she moved the vigour with which she was polishing up a gear. Molly remained silent, waiting for a response.

'I should have thrown those out the day he died,' she said eventually. 'They need burning.'

'Maybe you should keep the ones about the things that happened here in the house. It would be nice to frame them, maybe. They are real history. Visitors would be interested.'

'You're Alice's granddaughter, aren't you?' Mrs Woodcock changed the subject.

'Yes, do you know her?'

'She still alive?'

'Yes. She's ninety now. She doesn't leave the house much.'

'She was good to us when we were kids.'

'Us?'

'Me and him.' She nodded her head in the direction of the walled garden. 'She used to let us play around the farm; climbing on the hay bales, that sort of thing. Would have us in for tea and feed us cakes she'd made herself. Warm from the oven. She was a kind-hearted woman.'

'She's still in the same cottage,' Molly said. 'Not baking any more though.'

'Remember me to her,' Mrs Woodcock said.

'You should pop in to see her. She'd love that. She's a bit forgetful, doesn't always remember faces, but she still likes seeing people.'

'Losing a few memories isn't the worst thing that can happen to you,' Mrs Woodcock said. 'Some memories are not worth keeping hold of.'

'Do you mean those cuttings?' Molly tried again. 'Would you like me to take them off your hands? I could go through them and sort out the most interesting ones. The ones that might be worth keeping.'

Mrs Woodcock continued polishing as if Molly hadn't spoken, as if she had already left the room, already left the house. After a few more awkward, silent seconds, Molly decided she wasn't going to find out any more and returned to Trotsky, who spun with joy at her approach. She let him off his lead and he sped happily away on the scent of some invisible prey, as Molly walked back towards the gates. By the time she reached the village high street, Trotsky had not reappeared, so she balanced herself carefully on a half-rotted seat, which she remembered well from her childhood days of hanging out with friends after school had finished for the day, and called out Trotsky's name every so often, while flicking idly through her phone. It was the first day off she had given herself for several weeks and she was not sure what she should be doing with the empty hours. It was a disconcerting, guilty feeling.

'You have lost Trotsky?' A lightly accented woman's voice penetrated her thoughts and she looked up to find Daisy standing over her.

'He'll be back,' Molly said, 'as long as he hasn't got stuck down a rabbit hole.'

'That would be terrible.'

'Yes—' Molly refocused her brain away from her screen '—yes, I suppose it would. He used to do it all the time when he was young. He always managed to wriggle his way back out, but he is older and fatter these days.'

'Shall I help you to find him?'

'Um, okay. Thanks. I guess I should try to find him.' She glanced at her phone. 'He has been gone nearly an hour.'

They walked back into the grounds of the big house, calling out Trotsky's name as they went.

'So, where are you from?' Molly asked.

'France.'

'I guessed that. Whereabouts in France?'

'The south.'

'What brings you here?'

'Just a holiday.'

'But why here of all places? I mean, I know Mum and Dad are good landlords, but it's hardly a world-famous resort.'

'You like world-famous resorts?' Daisy asked. 'It is beautiful here. So peaceful. So picturesque. It's like a little forgotten world. The lovely colour of the stone that all the houses are built from. I find it very restful. The moss on the roofs. Beautiful views. Nice, funny people.'

'Yeah, all that, I guess,' Molly laughed, 'but you are still the only tourist in the entire village. People are curious.'

'I live on the coast, between Nice and Monaco,' Daisy said. 'During my life I have lived in Las Vegas, New York, Mustique. This is a good change from world-famous resorts.'

'I suppose it is.' Molly looked around her. 'I was born and brought up here. I guess I take it all for granted.'

'Well then, it is time that you opened your eyes, Molly, and looked around—' Daisy gestured at the surrounding panorama of fields, hills and trees, all dramatically visible now that the undergrowth had been cleared '—to see how lucky you are.'

'But still,' Molly persisted after a few moments' thought, and a few more tries at calling out Trotsky's name, 'how did you come to choose this village?'

'My mother was here once,' Daisy said, in a tone that suggested she was now trying to brush the whole subject away. 'Before I was born. She often talked about the village in England where she stayed, but I only recently found out the name.'

'Daisy is a pretty English-sounding name.'

'I was christened Marguerite. Daisy is the English translation. My mother liked it. It started as a nickname. Then Marc Jacobs created his perfume and now my name does not sound so typically English, I think.'

'The perfume is named after you?' Molly was impressed.

'I wouldn't exactly say that.' Daisy laughed, 'What about your family? Have they been here long?'

'Centuries, apparently. My grandfather used to be a tenant on one of the farms that were part of this estate. He inherited the lease from his father. It was right at the heart of the village. It was all sold off. All the barns have been converted into houses and cottages now.'

'All built from the same beautiful stone.'

'Exactly. My grandmother still lives in a cottage that was part of their farm, where the family had always lived. She and my grandfather got some sort of sitting tenancy when the farms were sold off, sometime in the seventies, I think. They got a payout from the Colonel, who lived here and owned most of the village. He didn't have any other farms to offer them, because he was selling all of them, so he put them into the pub as tenants, which my mum and dad run now.'

'A payout?' Daisy raised an eyebrow.

'Compensation for losing their livelihood on the farm, I guess.'

'So, they were your father's parents?'

'No, my mother's. My dad came to work there as a chef in the pub, that's how they met. "Valuable new bloodstock for the village" was how my gran described him.'

'Your grandmother sounds like a wise woman.'

Molly laughed. 'Sometimes. There's always a grain of truth in everything she says, even the maddest things.'

As they came closer to the big house, Molly noticed Benson stomping up the front steps, with Bryan trotting obediently at his heels.

'The old man seems to have trained that puppy quickly,' she said.

'He is a little bit brutal, I think,' Daisy said. 'I saw him hit the dog hard with a stick to make it obey. He hit too hard, I think.'

Molly was about to respond about the traditional ways of countryfolk when she saw Mrs Woodcock coming out of the front door, carrying the old leather suitcase that she and Zahara had found and handing it to Benson.

'She's getting him to burn it,' she said. The comment was more for herself.

'Burn what?'

'Stories. The history of the house. That suitcase is full of old newspaper articles.'

'Then perhaps we should stop him,' Daisy suggested, trying not to give away how anxious she too was to save any articles that might provide a glimpse into the history of the house. 'If you think they are important.'

'I don't know if they are important, but I would certainly like to spend some more time reading them before he destroys them.'

'I think you better run then,' Daisy said, following a few metres behind as Molly sprinted towards the walled garden, after the old man. Mrs Woodcock had disappeared back into the house.

'Hi,' Molly called out, as she got closer, 'Mr Benson. Have you got a minute?'

Bryan, recognising the woman who had brought him to his new life and new master, momentarily forgot his training and leapt joyously up to lick her face.

'Down!' Benson snarled, grabbing Bryan by the scruff of the neck and forcing all four paws back to the ground.

'It's okay,' Molly assured him, 'he's just being friendly. Please don't be angry with him.'

'What do you want?' Benson asked.

'That suitcase. Has Mrs Woodcock asked you to get rid of it?'

He stared at her for several moments, as if weighing up whether he wanted to say anything to her at all. She held her nerve and waited.

'Yes,' he replied eventually. 'I'm having a bonfire.'

'It's full of archive material about the house,' Molly said. 'I would really appreciate a chance to go through it before you burn it. Would that be possible?'

'Archive material?'

'Articles and things.'

Benson glanced over Molly's shoulder at Daisy, who was now loitering in the gate, giving a curt nod of recognition as Trotsky came barrelling in between her legs on his way to Bryan. Daisy smiled back and he averted his eyes.

'Bryan!' Benson roared as the Alsatian gave in to the temptation for a romp. 'Come!'

For a few seconds Bryan seemed torn between pleasing his new master and playing with his new friend. Deciding that Trotsky was the more attractive option, and that the possibility of a romp outweighed the potential beating that might follow, he crashed through the newly planted rose beds in pursuit. The fact that he seemed to be bleeding from several places did not slow Trotsky down as he ran tight circles round the bigger dog, yapping joyfully.

'Articles,' Benson said again, as if something was clicking into place in his memory, suddenly making sense to him. 'She would want to be rid of them. Too many bad memories.'

'Memories?'

'The Colonel used to cut them out of the newspapers and read them out at the breakfast table. Anything to frighten him into staying here, out of sight.'

'He'd read them to Bryan?' Molly wanted to be sure she was understanding what she was being told. 'To intimidate him into staying home?'

'That's what she told me.' He nodded towards the house. 'That's what her mother told her. Didn't want him out there, getting arrested again, drawing attention to himself, bringing the family name into disrepute.'

'Wow.' Molly was having trouble getting her head round what the old man was telling her. 'So, he used all that stuff to keep Bryan in self-imposed exile, for fear of being attacked, or being arrested and sent back to prison?'

'Or getting the disease.'

'AIDS?'

Benson nodded. 'In the end he was frightened of his own shadow, poor old boy.'

'And he let his father do that to him?'

'The Colonel was a very persuasive man.'

'Sounds like a bully to me,' Molly said.

'Take this if you want it so much,' Benson said, pushing the case into her arms with such force she almost toppled backwards, 'but don't tell her, and get that damn terrier out of here.'

'He's bleeding,' Molly said, noticing for the first time.

'Looks like he's had a set-to with a fox,' Benson said. 'They're getting to be bold as brass.'

As Molly hurried towards the gate in the wall, fearful that Mrs Woodcock might appear at any moment, barring her exit and demanding the return of the suitcase, Trotsky roared past at ground level, followed by Bryan. Daisy swept the small dog off his feet, his little legs pedalling frantically in mid-air, struggling to be free. His cuts left bright-red smears across the pale-grey wool of her coat, which Betty had already identified as being from Dior. The two women started to run as Benson came after his dog with a hastily snatched-up raspberry cane.

'I feel like Peter Rabbit,' Molly said, when they were at a safe enough distance to stop running and get their breath, putting Trotsky back on the lead. 'Being chased by Mr McGregor.'

'Mr McGregor?' Daisy sounded puzzled.

'Old English children's story,' Molly started to explain, but thought better of it. 'Don't worry about it.'

CHAPTER TWELVE

'Can I see some of these articles?' Daisy asked when they got back to the pub.

'Sure.' Molly shrugged, unsure whether old English newspaper stories would be particularly interesting for a French woman on holiday. 'Let's go in here.'

The snug was empty so she opened the case on the floor and divided the articles up into two piles, placing them on the table in front of them. 'Shall I see if I can rustle us up a pot of coffee?'

'That would be very nice,' Daisy said, her reading glasses already on the end of her nose as she sifted carefully through the brittle papers, aware of the grey inkiness spreading across the tips of her fingers.

'Mum!' Molly shouted over the bar in the direction of the kitchen. 'Can Daisy and I have a pot of coffee in the snug?'

Joan and her husband exchanged surprised looks at the news that when Daisy finally chose to socialise, it was with their daughter.

'OK,' she shouted back. 'I'll bring biscuits.'

By the time Joan came into the snug with a tray and laid out the coffee pot, cups and home-made biscuits, Molly and Daisy had sorted all the stories about Bryan's arrest at the big house into a separate pile. On the top of the pile was a front page from the *News of the World*. Under the headline 'Aristo Orgy in Country Pile' was a picture of Bryan and two other young men being escorted down the front steps of the house towards waiting police cars. The police uniforms and cars looked comically old-fashioned, like costumes and props from the age of black and white films.

'What happened to Trotsky?' Joan asked.

'Got into a fight with a fox, I think. Is he okay?'

'Doesn't seem too bothered, just licking his wounds all over the cushions in the bar. Looks like he bled on your coat.' She pointed to the dark stains on Daisy's otherwise immaculate coat. 'That'll be hard to shift.'

'Did you know about all this?' Molly asked her mother, gesturing to the newspaper story.

Joan took a second to read the first paragraph. 'I knew something like this went on up there, but it was long before my time. People used to gossip about it a bit when I was young, especially in here, when they'd had a few too many, but I didn't really understand what they were talking about. The house was quite notorious for a while – and the village too, I believe. And then in the sixties, there was the Profumo scandal at Cliveden and The Rolling Stones getting caught with drugs at Keith Richards' house, and I guess the newspapers forgot about us. I think Bryan's father did a good job of suppressing the story and making sure everything about the village was ultra-respectable from then on.'

'Gran would remember it all then?'

'Your grandmother never wanted to talk about anything to do with the big house. People always seemed to be very careful what they said when she was around, in case they got their heads bitten off. She was never a one for idle gossip.'

'Unusual for a publican,' Molly said, ducking out of reach of her mother's swinging tea-towel.

'I think she felt that the Toby family treated your grandfather badly when they sold off the farm,' Joan continued, her face serious again as she tried to recall things she hadn't thought about for many years. 'There was some very bad blood there, but I never got to the bottom of it. You could try asking her. She might be more willing to spill the beans to you. If she can remember now.'

Daisy looked up sharply from her reading and, for a moment, it seemed as if she was going to say something, but then she thought better of it and thanked Joan for the coffee instead, remarking on how delightful the biscuits looked and smelled.

'Daisy's mother visited the village a long time ago,' Molly said, feeling the need to include the French woman in the conversation.

'Really?' Joan couldn't hide her interest. 'When was that?'

'Oh, a little time after the war,' Daisy said. 'A long time ago. Before I was born.'

'We must have made a big impression,' Joan said, 'for you to come back after all these years.'

'Yes. She talked about the village a great deal. She always said how beautiful it was. Whenever we visited a picturesque village in France, in Provence or in the mountains, she would always say that it reminded her of her time in England.'

'That's nice to hear,' Joan said. 'I'll leave you two to it, then.'

'Maybe you should try asking your grandmother about all this,' Daisy said once Joan had left the room. 'It is good to hear the memories of the old people, before they are gone forever. Even the bad ones. There are so many things that I wish I had asked my mother.'

'I will. She probably would remember your mother. There can't have been that many French girls around at that time. What was her name?'

'Claudette.'

Joan's husband looked up enquiringly from the stove, where he was stirring a bubbling cauldron of vegetable soup, as she came back into the kitchen.

'Apparently her mother was here, just after the war. That's why she has come back. Some sort of pilgrimage, I guess.'

'Why was her mother here? Was she evacuated or something?'

Joan shrugged. 'No idea. But those two are getting on like a house on fire in there, so maybe Molly will find out more.'

Molly carefully brushed biscuit crumbs off an article from *The Times*, and pointed a paragraph out to Daisy. 'Bryan was sent to prison for twelve months, along with several of his friends. Imagine what a shock that would be to a young man like that, going from living in a place like this.'

'Terrible.' Daisy shivered dramatically. 'So young and good-looking, to be in prison would be very dangerous for him, I think. In France I believe we stopped punishing people for being gay during the Revolution.'

'A much healthier attitude to these sorts of things.'

Daisy laughed. 'Yes, I think so. We have a phrase, *"le vice anglais".*'

They both read in silence for a few minutes, nursing the warm coffee cups in their hands, sipping from time to time as if to comfort themselves.

'So, would your mother have been here at the time all this was happening at the house?'

Daisy didn't look up for a few moments, and Molly wondered if she had heard her.

'Yes, I believe so,' she said eventually. 'She was working at the house.'

'Working at the house? Doing what?'

'They had many horses. She looked after them.'

Molly stared at Daisy hard, trying to take in what she was saying. 'Like a groom?'

'I think so. She loved horses. She was married to a race horse trainer for a while. That was many years later, of course.'

'So, how long was she here?'

Daisy shrugged. 'A few years, I think she met him in Paris at the end of the war and he offered her a job.'

'Met who? Bryan?' Molly was beginning to sense that Daisy knew more about the background to the stories they were reading than she had been letting on.

'No, Bryan would have been just a boy in the war. His father.' She gestured to the articles. 'The one they call "the Colonel". I believe his name was Donald. Donald Toby. Colonel Donald Toby.' Daisy was no longer looking Molly in the eye. She was staring fixedly at the newspapers as she talked, as if she wanted to get back to reading, as if she didn't want to impart any more information than she had to. 'She never told me his name, but she said he was something to do with the British government, and she was part of the Free French Army.'

'The Resistance?'

'Something like that. She didn't like to talk about it and I didn't like to ask too many questions. The war was a hard time for her, I think. The Nazis executed both her parents. The invitation to come here to such a safe, peaceful place must have been very nice for her, I think. No?'

'So, how did you find out his name, if she never told you?'

'A well-wisher told me, so then I knew where to come. I wish I had asked her more when I was able to. You should talk to your grandmother, while you still have her here.'

They both went back to reading, lost in their own differing threads of thought.

CHAPTER THIRTEEN

Two days before she arrived at the Crown Inn, Daisy had been at home in Villefranche-sur-Mer, giving very little thought to her mother or to the past. In fact, she was taking her daily walk beside the Mediterranean, simply enjoying the warmth of the sun on her face and looking forward to a lunch party with friends who owned a villa out on Cap Ferrat, when her phone rang. She sat down on a bench to answer it as she gazed out at the boats. The caller's number was unknown to her.

'*Oui?*' she said, a little cautiously.

'Mademoiselle de Courcy?' The man's voice had an English accent, but sounded forthright and professional.

'Who is asking?' Daisy replied in English.

'My name is Gerald Remers. We have never met. Please forgive me calling out of the blue like this. I am a lawyer and one of my clients is an Englishman called Bryan Toby. I should say, "was" an Englishman called Bryan Toby.'

'Yes?' Daisy's heartbeat quickened, but her tone gave nothing away. It felt as if she had been waiting all her life for a call to come from England, but still it had taken her by surprise when it finally arrived.

'Rather a delicate matter has arisen and I wondered if I might meet you in order to explain the situation.'

'A delicate matter?'

'Yes, very delicate. I wouldn't wish to discuss it over the phone. And I am not sure that it would be appropriate for me to put anything in writing.'

'I see,' Daisy said, although she didn't.

'I believe that you have a residence in Villefranche?'

'I do.'

'It so happens that I am at my apartment in Menton. Could I suggest that we meet somewhere convenient to both of us? I would be delighted to buy you lunch somewhere. Perhaps the Hotel Paris in Monaco? Do you know it?'

'Yes.' Daisy couldn't imagine there were many people of her age on the Riviera who did not know the Hotel Paris, standing proud, as it did, across the square from the infamous Casino de Monte-Carlo.

'Would you join me there for lunch tomorrow at Ducasse's restaurant?'

'I would be delighted.'

'Would one o'clock be good?'

'Yes, of course.'

· · ·

The following day, Gerald was already waiting at a table in one of the windows when the head waiter led her across the golden, glowing room, beneath the soaring painted ceiling. Her host was so immaculately dressed in a pale-blue linen suit, his neatly trimmed, snow-white hair swept back from a high, darkly tanned forehead, that it was a few minutes before she realised he must be very old, his skin as thin as ancient parchment, dappled with liver spots beneath the tan.

They made careful, polite small talk about how much Monaco had changed for the worse over the previous half century, until they had ordered their food, and each had a drink standing in front of them.

'I believe I knew your mother,' he said. 'Before you were born. I was so sorry to learn that she had passed away.'

'Thank you. It was a car crash,' Daisy said. 'She always drove too fast. It was the same road where Princess Grace died. Those mountain bends can be so treacherous. You say you knew her?'

She stared at him hard, trying to imagine what he would have looked like seventy years ago, searching for anything in his features that might be recognisable in her own DNA.

'Yes. Many, many years ago. I was still a student, at Oxford. I used to stay with Bryan Toby's family a great deal. A lot of us did. Most of us went to school together as well. Your mother was also there. Working for the family, I believe. She was a very striking woman, and a strong personality. She made a powerful impression on us callow English youths. She had exciting tales to tell, about her time working for the Resistance when she was a teenager. In my memory she looked a little like Brigitte Bardot.'

'They were a similar age.' Daisy smiled at the memory. 'My mother a little older, perhaps. They were good friends. Simone de Beauvoir wrote about them.'

'I remember.' Gerald seemed lost in his own memories for a moment. 'But we knew your mother before she became famous. She was still a young girl, really.'

'Yes,' Daisy said. 'She told me that she took care of the horses for a family. She never told me the name of the family, just that she had spent some years in England before I was born. Bryan Toby, you say? That is the name?'

Gerald nodded thoughtfully, apparently reluctant to give out any more information until he had collected more from her. 'Tell me about your father, my dear,' he said after a moment. 'If you don't mind me asking.'

'My father?' She was shocked by such a blunt, personal question from someone who seemed so meticulously polite. 'Do you mean my stepfather? And if so, which one? My mother married several times.'

'Were these stepfathers kind to you?' It sounded as if he was genuinely concerned as to what sort of childhood she might have had. Was he showing a paternal interest, she wondered.

'Some more than others,' she replied, after only a moment's hesitation. 'It was a long time ago. Men will be men, you know.'

Her heart was thumping uncomfortably hard and she was finding it difficult to breathe. She was keen to steer the conversation back to her mother's time in England, but did not wish to seem impolite. She didn't want to frighten him away from whatever revelation he might be contemplating making, by being too forward and giving the impression of indiscretion.

'I'm sorry to hear that,' he said. 'I was actually thinking about your biological father.'

'Him I didn't know. Maman always wanted me to think of her husbands as my fathers, which was difficult when she kept changing them.'

Gerald seemed entirely unsurprised by what he was hearing. He obviously knew a lot more about her mother's past than she did, and seemed to be trying to find out what she knew before saying something that might prove indiscreet. Perhaps, she thought, he wanted to find out how she felt about her absent father, whether she bore any grudges. before confessing who he was.

'You were happy with that arrangement?'

'I was willing to accept it as a child. When you are little, you assume that everyone lives the same way as you, no? But as an adult, I have often felt curious about who my real father might be, but I never wanted to upset Maman by asking too many questions. She obviously didn't want to talk about it. I feel perhaps she did not even want to think about it. I thought it had been unrequited love, a broken heart, and she found it too painful to remember. I imagined sometimes that the reason she married so many times, why she was so restless, always seeking love, was that the love of her life had escaped her in England. It was a romantic story, which I constructed for myself, with no facts at all.'

'Would you like to know more facts?'

'Are you in a position to tell me more?'

'I believe I am.'

Exquisitely prepared food was placed in front of them, and the wine that Gerald had selected was poured into their glasses.

'Yes,' she said, once the waiter had withdrawn, after giving a painfully long, reverentially hushed explanation about every item that was on their plates. 'I would like to know more about my father.'

'Your father was Colonel Donald Toby, my friend Bryan's father. He was in Paris at the end of the war and he met your mother there. He must have found out that she wanted to work with horses and he invited her to England, offering her a job in the stables at his house. I believe she had lost both her parents a few years before, so perhaps she was grateful to be included in a new family. I believe both your grandparents were in the Resistance as well.'

'Yes,' she said. 'They were caught and executed. I think it affected her badly.'

She felt strangely disappointed to discover that the man she was lunching with was not her father, but at the same time excited to finally have a name, and access to someone who could tell her more.

'Presumably he was married to Bryan's mother,' she said after a few moments' thought, forcing herself to remain calm and holding back the tears that wanted to spring free. The immaculate food stood, ignored, in front of her.

'Indeed. Not a faithful man.'

'So, your friend, Bryan, is my half-brother?'

'Was your half-brother. I'm afraid he passed away yesterday.'

'Yesterday? That is a shame. It would have been nice to know about him while he was still alive, while we could still meet.'

'He was a man who was burdened with a great many secrets.'

'And you helped him to guard those secrets?'

'I helped him with financial matters, finding ways to raise money so that he could continue living in his family's house long after he could realistically afford it. I always felt that I owed him a great debt. I would do anything to help him. I might advise him to share the burden with others, but if he insisted that it was his alone to bear, then I would honour his wishes, always.'

'Until now.'

'Indeed. Until now. I am a very old man, like Bryan; if I die then I believe the secrets will die with me.'

'Which is what Bryan would have wanted?'

'Perhaps.'

'But you think he was wrong?'

'I do. After a great deal of thought on the matter, over a very long period. I have had your phone number for several years. Bryan often talked of your mother, and wondered what became of her, so I tracked her down. Tracked both of you down. I always planned to contact you if he passed away before me. I am the executor of his will. He would have liked to leave you something, but there is nothing, other than enormous debts, which are far bigger than the value of the house where he died, which he has left to those who have also lived there all their lives. Something of a poisoned chalice for them, I'm afraid. For many years it has been very hard putting together deals that would create the cash flow he needed to stay on in the house. Each year the debts grew bigger and harder to negotiate. They compounded, you could say, at a frightening rate. I would not have been able to keep it up for much longer. My sole aim was to allow him the comfort of dying in his own bed.'

'And you succeeded?'

'I did, but at a terrible cost to his family's estate.' Gerald gave a thin smile. 'Your family's estate. There is nothing left.'

Daisy stirred her food around the plate with a fork while she gathered her thoughts.

'Thank you for telling me this,' she said eventually. 'It is nice to know that he remembered my mother, and knew of my existence. The money is not important. I have plenty, and no dependents. I certainly wouldn't want to be responsible for a house in England. I need only a pied-à-terre with a view of the Mediterranean, which is what I have.'

Gerald, looking relieved by her reaction, placed a minute, carefully selected forkful of food between his lips.

'How did you become so indebted to a friend that you would do so much for him?' she asked.

'Many, many years ago, we were both arrested for something that is no longer considered a crime in most countries.' He paused, staring into her eyes, giving her time to nod that she understood what he was saying. 'He, and several of our friends, ended up in prison for a year, but my family exerted their influence and I received no punishment, beyond feeling guilty about those who did, including, and principally, Bryan.

They suffered greatly, particularly Bryan. I was immensely fond of him.' She heard his voice catch as if the memory had constricted his throat. He struggled to swallow the morsel of food. 'My father was a cabinet minister. Many influential people hoped that he would one day become prime minister. They did not want his son to have a prison record.'

'And Bryan's father was not influential?'

'He could have influenced the way things went, perhaps, but he chose not to.'

'So, you are telling me that my father was not a very good father?'

'They were different times, but he and Bryan did not have a comfortable relationship, no.'

Daisy chewed a small mouthful in silence for a few minutes as she tried to work out how she felt. 'My mother and Bryan would have been around the same age.'

'That is correct.'

'So, Donald Toby slept with a girl who was the same age as his son?'

'I am not certain that "slept together" is quite the right term for what happened.'

'He raped her?'

'Well—' Gerald was obviously embarrassed by the news he was sharing '—the two people who could answer that question for certain are both dead. But it is possible that your mother was not the only young girl who ended up in this position.'

'He was a serial rapist? How on earth would you know that?'

'Once Bryan came home from prison, his father didn't care what he saw or heard. He had nothing but contempt for him. He thought more of his horses and dogs than his son. Bryan confided some of the things he knew to me.'

'But what about Bryan's mother?'

'I suspect she chose not to know. A lot of wives did in those days. She had her own interests.'

'Such arrangements are not unheard of in France either.' Daisy smiled. 'So, do I have other half-brothers and half-sisters?'

'I believe so. Bryan believed so.'

'Do any of them know who their father was?'

'That I don't know.' He looked directly at her. 'Have I done the right thing in telling you these things? I hope I have.'

'Yes,' she nodded. 'You have done the right thing. Tell me more about the people who have inherited the house, the ones who have lived there all their lives.'

'I don't know very much. I knew their parents, but only as staff, who were always in the background, making the place run like clockwork. They were children when I was last there. Delightful children, I seem to remember, full of life but very well brought up and polite to their elders. I'm planning to go there in a couple of days, to let them know the situation and perhaps to advise on what they can do about the debts, should they want advice from someone who will doubtless seem like a stranger to them.'

'He still had live-in staff, even after the money had run out?'

'I'm afraid they have not been paid anything for many, many years. Like him, they lived for free in the house, and we managed to generate enough cash flow to feed everyone, keep a car on the road, pay the electricity bills, that sort of thing. But certainly not enough for anyone to receive any salary.'

Daisy stared at him hard for a few moments, trying to piece together everything she was learning. 'Their mothers worked in the house at the same time as my mother? And they would be the same sort of age as me?'

Gerald looked momentarily flustered, as if he had been tricked into giving away more than he should have done.

'Yes,' he said, with a rueful smile. 'They would be contemporaries of yours.'

'I would like to meet them,' she said. 'It sounds like we might have a great deal in common.'

'Why don't we go together? I have booked to stay in the pub in the village. It used to be part of the Toby estate, in the days when they owned the whole village, but I helped Bryan to sell it to the tenants some years back, when he first started needing cash. Would you like me to book a room for you too?'

'I think I would like to be anonymous, at least to start with, until I have decided if it would be appropriate to intro-duce myself. I might decide, perhaps, that it would be better to let sleeping dogs lie. That is an English expression, no?'

'It is indeed. Very wise of you. But I think there is only the one pub in the village.'

'I will try to get a room there then, but perhaps we won't admit that we know each other. It might make things complicated.'

'Of course. I understand. If I see you there, I will be discreet. I shall feel like James Bond.'

'I think that would be best.' Daisy smiled, suddenly excited at the prospect of finally finding some of her paternal family. 'And what about your father? Did he become prime minister?'

'No,' Gerald laughed, 'he did not. As it turned out, it would have made no difference if his son was a jailbird. So, they wasted all their efforts, didn't they?'

CHAPTER FOURTEEN

Daisy had decided it was wiser to make a return visit to the big house without Trotsky. He had served his purpose as an ice-breaker, and now ran the risk of merely being a distraction. As she came into the walled garden, Bryan looked up at his master for permission before greeting her. Benson did not give it, keeping his head down and continuing to fiddle with the rose bushes, which now stretched out in long, tightly regimented lines along the newly dug and freshly nourished beds. The workforce who had planted them had moved on to other parts of the estate, returning him a small piece of his former tranquillity.

'They should make a beautiful show next year for the wedding,' Daisy said, but Benson didn't respond. 'I have not brought the dog today,' she said, but there was still no reaction. 'Please may I speak to you and Mrs Woodcock together? Perhaps we could go to the house? It is a delicate matter.'

After several moments the old man straightened up, gave his back a rub and stared straight at her.

'You want to talk to her?'

'I do. And I want to talk to you. It is a delicate matter.' She repeated Gerald's phrase.

'She can help you with whatever you need. You've no need to talk to me. She doesn't like me going inside the house.'

'Please.' Daisy was not going to be put off by his abrupt manner. She was well used to handling churlish men. 'It is something that is important to all of us.'

'All of us?' He was beginning to sound irritated. She remembered how hard he had thrashed the dog and took a precautionary step back.

'Please,' she said again, uncomfortably aware that, unlike most of the men she aimed her gaze at, he did not seem to find her charming in any way.

He dropped his secateurs into the trug with a loud crack. 'Stay!' he instructed Bryan, who flattened himself out on the ground with a resentful curl of his black lip. 'Come on then,' he grunted, walking ahead of her through the wall, towards the house. He did not look back as she hurried after him.

Mrs Woodcock did not appear pleased to see them as Benson led the way in through the kitchen door. She glanced down at the mud dropping from his boots, but decided not to say anything until she had him on his own.

'She says she wants to talk to us,' he announced, plumping himself down at the kitchen table and setting about rolling himself a cigarette.

'May I sit?' Daisy asked and Mrs Woodcock shrugged, which Daisy took to be permission.

'My mother worked here in the early fifties,' she said, watching as they exchanged uncomfortable glances. 'She worked in the stables, with the horses. She had to return to France because she became pregnant with me.'

Mrs Woodcock said nothing, choosing to ignore Benson, who had set light to his roll-up, something she had ordered him not to do in her kitchen countless times over the years. She was not comfortable with the way everything was sliding out of her control around her. Why did this woman want to come back to the house now? Was she a threat? Did she have some sort of legal claim over the estate? Was she going to lie to them about the past? Thank goodness Bryan was not here, to have his peace of mind disturbed so unexpectedly.

'She was raped by Donald Toby,' Daisy said. 'So, he was my father.'

'Anyone can claim they were raped by someone who is long dead. He can hardly deny it from the grave,' Mrs Woodcock snapped. 'I don't believe a word of it.'

Daisy could see from their faces that they both could believe it.

'I have a confession to make to you,' Daisy continued. 'I have undertaken a DNA test. Bryan and I undoubtedly shared a parent.'

'How would you have Bryan's DNA?' Mrs Woodcock asked, with a note of triumph in her voice, as if she had exposed the fake claimant in one blow.

'That is what I must confess,' Daisy said. 'I took a hairbrush and a toothbrush from his room.'

'Sounds like daylight robbery to me,' Benson muttered, without removing the roll-up from his lower lip.'

'I know,' Daisy said, 'I am sorry.'

'Police might be interested to hear about that,' he continued.

'Maybe it wasn't rape.' Mrs Woodcock's voice was rising. 'You know what young French girls are like.'

'Flirty,' Benson suggested, spitting a stray flake of tobacco onto the freshly washed floor.

'Exactly,' Mrs Woodcock agreed, willing to ignore the spitting in exchange for his moral support against a common enemy.

'She was the same age as Bryan,' Daisy persevered with her story. 'Not much more than a teenager. Donald Toby was her employer. Her married employer. I have been told that he was known to be a ladies' man.'

'Told by whom?'

'Someone who knew the family well.'

'That doesn't mean he went round raping young girls.'

'I think he did it a lot,' Daisy said.

'Hold on a minute.' Mrs Woodcock now sounded angry enough to lash out. 'You've got no right to come in here, accusing people of things you can't prove.'

'I believe he raped both your mothers in the same year that he raped mine.'

A blanket of silence descended on the kitchen as her words sunk in. Mrs Woodcock felt the anger subside in her. She began to shiver and pushed her hands into the pockets of her apron so that the others wouldn't see that they were shaking, although Benson's stare had become fixed on the table-top, as if he didn't want to see or hear anything that was happening in the room.

Pictures flashed inside Mrs Woodcock's head as she tried to steady her breathing. She remembered the surprising strength of the old man's hands as he forced her down onto her knees and pushed his thick fingers between her teeth to prise open her mouth. She remembered how sour they tasted. She remembered his cries of encouragement, 'Come on, young filly! There you go! Good girl!' She remembered thinking she was going to choke and blaming herself for ignoring her mother's strict instructions and straying into his study unchaperoned. As soon as he had finished, and dismissed her with a friendly smack on the backside, she had run to the top of the house to hide and recover, and that was where Bryan had found her, and had held her while she'd sobbed, and had said kind words to her.

'Your mothers were both around the same age as mine.' Daisy spoke again, startling Phyllis back into the room. 'Both working in the house at that time. They all fell pregnant at around the same time. I believe we are all roughly the same age.'

The roll-up burned brightly as Benson inhaled the smoke to the deepest corners of his lungs.

'Are you suggesting we are all the Colonel's children?' Mrs Woodcock asked, as if wanting to be sure she had understood everything correctly, leaving no margin for error or misunderstanding.

Daisy nodded. 'Would you both be willing to take DNA tests?'

'You think Bryan believed all this?' Benson asked.

'I do,' Daisy said. 'I think that is why he left you everything.'

'Everything and nothing,' Benson muttered.

'Is that why you are here?' Mrs Woodcock asked. 'To stake your claim?'

'No. I have all the money I need. I just wanted to meet my family. Maybe we could get to know one another.'

Both Benson and Mrs Woodcock looked puzzled at the idea that they would want to get to know anyone new.

'A little saliva,' Daisy said, trying not to look too closely at the crusts of phlegm resting in the stubble at the corners of Benson's mouth. 'That's all I need from you. Wouldn't you like to know the truth?'

'The Colonel may have raped your mother,' Mrs Woodcock said. 'I don't know anything about that. But our fathers were kind, decent men. Why would we want to find out anything different? I've got better things to do with my time than listen to this nonsense.' She stood up to indicate the discussion was over. 'I don't want to hear another word about it. And you, Tom Benson, can take your muddy boots back out into the garden and all!'

CHAPTER FIFTEEN

'We've had an anonymous call, Mr Benson,' the young policewoman said, once she had persuaded Benson to let her in through his cottage door. 'A man with a foreign accent.'

Benson could see that she was shocked by the state of his kitchen and the precariously piled books on every surface. If he had known she was coming, he would have made sure he was outside when she arrived. He didn't like anyone penetrating his private space, but he hadn't stepped outside the cottage since returning from hearing what the French woman had to say earlier that day. He was not feeling himself at all, and did not welcome another unexpected visit. At the same time, he was tempted by the distraction from his own thoughts that the young woman's arrival was allowing him.

'Plenty of foreigners around here these days,' he muttered, gesturing towards the walled garden. 'God knows where they are all from.'

'Sounded Eastern European,' she said, sitting down without an invitation, eyeing the state of the sink and the cooker, hoping the old man wouldn't offer to make her a cup of tea, but intrigued to know more about him.

'You live here on your own?' she asked.

'I do,' he said, before nodding towards Bryan, who had settled back down in front of the age-stained Rayburn. 'Apart from him.'

'He's beautiful.'

'He stinks,' Benson chuckled. 'Rolled in some fox shit earlier.'

'Oh, is that what the smell is?'

'Did you think it was me?' He chuckled again, this time at her discomfort.

'How long have you been living here?' she asked, eager to change the subject.

'I was born here,' he said, nodding towards the ceiling. 'Upstairs. Been here ever since.'

'You've never been anywhere else?'

'There's always been plenty to do here.'

'Never wanted to try something else? See the world?' She seemed genuinely interested.

'Thought about joining the Army once,' he said, shocked to find he was talking so openly to a stranger. His thoughts had become muddled since hearing what the French woman had to say, with all sorts of memories bubbling back to the surface. It felt surprisingly helpful to talk to someone, to a stranger. 'So I could "see the world". It's the only time my old man got really angry with me. "The Army is just people like him, sending people like us to kill other people like us, or be killed while trying." That's what he said, and he was right. I came to see that well enough for myself.'

'Who did he mean by "people like him"? The old boy who died the other day in the big house?'

'Not Bryan, no. His father, the Colonel. The Colonel enjoyed his war. Revelled in people calling him "Colonel". Never saw a shot fired in anger, mind, but still believed he'd liberated France single-handedly. Bryan didn't go in for any of that.'

'Any of what?' she asked, her eyes scanning the spines of the books piled in front of her.

'He didn't believe in nationalism, patriotism and all that. He believed in respecting every individual equally, not a flag or a king or a queen. He said if you didn't have patriotism, the leaders wouldn't be able to start wars the way they do. He was ahead of his time.'

'A pacifist?' There was a hint of contempt in her voice, but Benson was enjoying talking for once and let it pass.

'Suppose he was, although he was never put to the test. My dad was, after being made to do National Service and being sent to Kenya and being ordered to kill and torture the Mau Mau in their own country. "They were just people like us," he used to say, "wanting their land back so that they could feed their families. All property is theft." That's what my dad used to say. "And land owners are the biggest thieves of all." The Colonel was a land owner, you see. I guess he was a communist.'

'The Colonel?'

'My dad,' Benson chuckled. 'Definitely not the Colonel. My dad thought the whole system was corrupt, but he felt he was trapped in it. The Colonel gave him just enough in the way of security to make it hard to leave, but in the end, he owned nothing. He might as well have been a slave.'

'But you're still here as well,' the young woman pointed out.

Benson nodded. 'Bryan was different. He never bossed anyone about. He never shouted at anyone, or threatened anyone or forced his attentions on anyone. He wasn't trying to impress with his achievements or his possessions. He just wanted to be left alone to read his books and think his thoughts. That suited me just fine. I guess you could call him a pacifist. He didn't even want to wage war on the pheasants. The Colonel used to run this big shoot. Well, my dad ran it for him. The Colonel would invite his friends, most of whom would invite him back to their own shoots at their family estates, and they would bag thousands of birds in a day. It was quite a sight. I used to do the beating for them when I was a kid. A lot of the kids from the village did. There would be dozens of these idiots firing away, bodies raining down from the sky, dogs running around all over the place, the women joining them for picnic lunches, big tables covered in food and drink. Bryan put a stop to all that.'

'He was a vegetarian as well as a pacifist?'

'No, he didn't mind killing things if they were going to be eaten. But these toffs were just killing things to prove they could, just to show what "jolly good shots" they were.' Benson chuckled at his own impression of the sort of people he had spent his life silently serving. 'Towards the end, the old man needed more money and he used to charge these city types thousands of pounds to spend the day pretending they were country gentry, quaffing champagne in the woods, wearing brand-new tweeds and wellington boots that cost hundreds of pounds, talking about their guns in the same way they talked about their fancy cars, all trying to outdo everyone else, boasting about how much money they had. Bryan wasn't having any of that once he took control. He always said "no one needs money that badly".'

'So, what happens now he's died?'

Benson shrugged, but didn't reply. The young police-woman was about to ask more about the past, but remembered she was supposed to be there in an official capacity and pulled out her notebook.

'You look after the grounds?' she asked.

'I do.'

'So, you hire all the foreign workers?'

'I do not. They're to do with this wedding business up at the house. I've been managing perfectly well on my own for nearly forty years.'

She consulted her notebook. 'This caller said they were turning up a load of bones. He said we should take a look.'

For a second, she thought she saw a frown flicker over the old man's sun-dried face.

'So, you want to know where the bodies are buried?' he said, relighting his roll-up and dropping the match into a nearly empty coffee cup, where it fizzled loudly.

'Bodies?'

'Plenty of them to be found. Foxes bring them up all the time.'

'Foxes?' The young woman seemed perplexed.

'Everywhere. They're everywhere since he did away with the hunt. Clearing away the undergrowth has brought them back out into the open. Bold as brass.'

'Could we have a look at these bones?' she asked, keen to get back into the fresh air and away from the smell of the brown stains embedded in Bryan's fur.

'You can. I told them to dig them back in, but they haven't done it. Just piled them up. But there's plenty more where they came from.'

'You told them to bury them again?'

'They're good for the soil.'

'Bones are good for the soil?'

'Carcasses are good for the soil. The worms love 'em. The foxes love the worms. You see how it works?'

She snapped her notebook shut, her colour rising, suspecting she was being teased and patronised simultaneously. Was she dealing with a psychopathic serial killer, or just an old man with a warped sense of humour?

'I believe my colleagues were up here a week or two ago.'

Benson relit his cigarette, which had once more smouldered to a halt, and said nothing. Another match went into the coffee dregs.

'Responding to a report of a suspicious death.'

'We've all got to die sometime. He was over ninety years old. There was nothing suspicious. Unless you think she poisoned him with her cooking.' He chuckled again at his own joke.

'Do you have any reason to suspect Mrs Woodcock would have wanted to poison him?'

'She's always had a mean streak, that one,' Benson said, a twinkle in his eye as he watched the young policewoman's expression intensify as she reopened her notebook. 'We'd both been eating her terrible cooking for a good few years, so I imagine we were pretty immune to anything she might serve up.' He was suddenly tired of teasing the girl. 'She took good care of him. I dare say she kept him alive a long way past his allotted span.'

She looked up from her notes again. 'There was a report of an illegal firearm in the house.'

'It was just the Colonel's old pistol. He brought it back from the war. Forgot to hand it in. Or maybe didn't believe that law applied to him. Your colleagues took it away with them.'

'Apparently, it was in very good working order.'

'She keeps everything in the house in perfect working order, I'll say that for her. Even better than when her mother was alive, and her mother had God knows how many girls working for her.'

The policewoman consulted her notebook again. 'So, Mrs Woodcock looks after everything inside the house?'

'Yep. She looks after the inside. I look after the outside. That way, we don't have to see too much of one another.'

'And that gun?' She nodded towards the shotgun resting beside the door. 'I assume you have a licence for that?'

'Bryan took care of all the paperwork,' Benson grunted. 'It will be up at the house. She'll show you if you ask.'

'It should be in a locked cupboard.'

Benson pretended not to hear, so she made another note instead.

'So,' she said after a few moments, raising her voice to ensure he heard, 'the bones being dug up in the walled garden, then …'

'What about them?'

'Maybe we should take a look, Mr Benson.'

Benson nodded and expelled a shrill whistle through his teeth, waking Bryan up from his place beside the old Rayburn and bringing him to heel as the three of them walked up to the walled garden, the girl taking several deep gulps of fresh air. Standing in the gate, they surveyed the beds. She noted that there was a startling neatness compared to the gardens they had just walked through, which were still in the process of being cleared and the debris burnt.

'Someone has gone to a lot of trouble to tidy this all up, Mr Benson,' she said.

'Like a crime scene, you mean?'

Rose bushes stretched out in every direction, planted in lines of military precision. In the far corner of the wall was a neat pile of what looked like rubble. Benson waited with apparent indifference for her to focus her eyes on the pile and see that it was largely made up of bones. She walked over and peered more closely.

'These are bones.'

'Good work, Sherlock. I told you they were.' He was surprised to find he was enjoying the girl's company. Over the previous ten years he had come to believe that he hated all company. It was pleasant to find out that might not be true.

'And there are more buried in the beds, you say?' She had a horrible feeling he was flirting with her.

'Yep.'

'So, how do you explain so many bones?' she asked.

Benson shrugged. 'There's been a lot of animals over the years.'

'Animals?'

'Dogs mainly. A few cats. Several horses. The ponies Bryan's mother bought for him when he was a boy.'

She looked at the pile again, stirring it with her foot. 'Maybe the RSPCA would like to take a look then,' she said.

If she was hoping to unsettle the old man in order to make him more talkative, she was disappointed, because he almost laughed again.

'Can't imagine why they would, after all these years.'

'All these years since what?' she asked, but he didn't bother to reply. Instead, he gave another whistle and walked back to the cottage, with Bryan trotting beside him. If there was one day in his life that he didn't want to think about, let alone talk about, it was that one. The policewoman considered following him and asking more questions, but then she remembered how bad the kitchen had smelled and decided she had enough material to write a convincing report for her bosses.

CHAPTER SIXTEEN

It was a winter's evening when it happened. Benson was in the cottage, having got the fire blazing for his parents, who were huddled either side of the flames, only half awake, when there was an explosion of angry banging on the door and he heard the fearful sound of the Colonel's voice outside, raised in uncontrolled fury. He was tired because he had been up since five and had only just stopped work. He had found it hard to sleep since his parents had become sick. All his life he had worked alongside them both on the estate, living together in the tiny cottage. Now that Old Benson wasn't able to tell him what to do because of the stroke, he worried that he would forget something crucial, or would get to the end of the day and would have run out of time for all his allotted duties. His father might not be able to speak, but his disapproving looks could be withering. So, Benson made a point of rising as soon as he woke, and started each day by exercising the hounds.

His father had always seemed to be at his most contented when they were looking after the hounds, and Benson was coming to share that feeling. He was proud of the fact that it was known to be one of the best packs in the country, and several of the dogs had managed to single themselves out as favourites. His father had been worried about their future once the Colonel had gone. Keeping that many dogs was expensive and the Colonel was known to pay for much of it personally, just in order to keep the hunt going. Without him, no one knew what would happen.

'It's a country tradition,' his father explained to him when the angry taunts of the anti-hunt protestors had raised questions in Benson's mind, 'city people don't understand.'

Benson had tried on several occasions to point out that Bryan didn't approve of the practice either, but his father always pretended not to hear. Far from discouraging the Colonel, the protestors merely seemed to heighten his hunting instincts, as he whipped his horses on to ride straight through them, often drawing blood from both the horses and the protestors. The resulting court cases had been equally ineffective at denting his determination to gallop and jump wherever and whenever he chose, especially if it resulted in one less fox at the end of the day.

Benson always tried to stay out of the way when the Colonel was angry, particularly since the old man's back operation had stopped him from riding, making his temper even more easily ignited. His self-pitying frustration at having his greatest pleasures gradually eroded was a stark contrast to the quiet stoicism of Benson's mother, as she hobbled through her days on increasingly arthritic joints. That evening he sounded louder and more dangerous than Benson had ever heard him before. He hurried to open the door but the Colonel burst in before he could get there. Benson could see Bryan standing behind his father on the doorstep, too polite to enter another man's house uninvited. The Colonel was brandishing his revolver and his breath smelt of Scotch.

Benson's mother did not take her eyes off the flames in the fireplace, rubbing her permanently bent, nubbly fingers, trying in vain to keep the pain moving. It was as if she could not hear any of the shouting, as if she had put herself in another world. Benson had never seen her look at the Colonel, ever. Nor had he ever heard them exchange a word, unless it was the Colonel issuing a direct command to do with her duties, helping Philly's mother, cleaning the house. In the past he had often overheard his mother berating his father for being too eager to doff his cap to their employer. His father never responded to her goading, so Benson had come to assume there was nothing serious to worry about in their relationship. Mutual irritation was just the natural order of things.

'We need the keys to the kennels,' the Colonel roared.

'Yes, Colonel,' Benson replied.

'And you can come and help us.'

'Yes, sir.'

He had no idea what he was being asked to help with, but he could see how unhappy Bryan was about the situation. He was cradling a box in his arms as if it were an unexploded bomb. Benson thought he might have been crying. The Colonel's eyes rested for a second on the pile of paperbacks sitting on the kitchen table, waiting to be read, and his lip curled like a dog's snarl as he turned on his heel and headed back to the door.

'Because he's no fucking use to man nor beast,' he bellowed, punching his son out of the way with the fist that was gripping the gun and limping towards the kennels without looking back.

Benson glanced at Bryan in the hope of receiving a clue as to what was going on, before hurrying after his employer, clutching the required keys to the padlock, but Bryan just stared at the ground and followed the other two men without saying a word.

'They're going to have to go,' the Colonel announced as Benson unlocked the chains that held the gates and the clumsy, muscular hounds surged forward, excited by this unexpected late-night visit, hopeful that it meant they were going to be allowed out to follow the many exciting night-time scents that filled their bony heads, apparently pushing out all other thoughts.

'Can't afford to keep a pack if they aren't even going to work for a living. This pathetic idiot has made it clear that he wants nothing to do with any of it, and I'm all but finished. So, they have to go.'

Still not fully grasping what was happening, Benson pushed the eager, welcoming dogs back to allow the three of them further into the pen, worried that they might topple the unsteady Colonel over in his inebriated state, aware that the gun was almost certainly loaded and liable to go off at any moment.

'Bring them through to the food store one at a time,' the Colonel instructed as he threw open the store-room door and pushed Bryan in ahead of him. 'This is your doing! Now you have to face the consequences!'

Benson brought the first hound into the store room in a daze, finally able to guess what the Colonel was intending, but not quite believing that he would actually be able to carry out his threat. Maybe he was just trying to scare his son into changing his mind about hunting. It had been common knowledge on the estate for years that Bryan was not comfortable with the concept, and he had never shown the remotest interest in riding once his mother had given up trying to get him to enjoy Pony Club. It did not occur to Benson for a second to disobey the Colonel's orders, particularly when he was armed, angry and drunk.

'Close the door!' the Colonel ordered.

Benson obeyed and in the small, closed room, the sound of the revolver's first shot was deafening.

'Get this one out and bring the next,' the Colonel commanded, handing the revolver to his son as Benson dragged the first corpse back outside, leaving a trail of blood in his wake. His hearing temporarily drowned out, Benson could still read the words on the old man's foam-flecked lips.

The other dogs had fallen quiet, and came forward cautiously to sniff the corpse of their fallen comrade. Benson grabbed another by the scruff and pulled him into the room. He could only work like a robot. He couldn't stop to think. There was nothing he could do. Bryan was now holding the revolver and had put down the box, which Benson could see was full of ammunition.

'Just do it!' the Colonel shouted. 'You fucking useless pansy!'

For a second, Benson thought Bryan was going to appeal to him for help and he thought that perhaps the two of them together would be able to prevail against one drunk old man, but Bryan averted his eyes and pulled the trigger. The dog staggered and whimpered but didn't die.

'For Christ's sake! Fifty years old and you can't even fucking shoot straight!' The Colonel grabbed the gun and finished the job. 'Next!'

He was shouting at the top of his voice but Benson could barely hear anything over the ringing in his ears. He understood now what was expected of him. There was no point trying to stop the process now it was under way, no point saving some of the dogs if he couldn't save all of them. And if the hunt was being disbanded, they would probably have to be put down anyway.

'Bury them tomorrow,' the Colonel ordered as he limped out of the kennels nearly an hour later, apparently a little more sober than when he arrived. Bryan followed behind, his body shaking, his cheeks streaked with tears and the blood of the dogs. By the time Benson got back to the cottage, the flames of the fire had died to little more than a smoulder, but his mother had not moved, having merely pulled more blankets over herself and her husband, who was staring into the glowing embers. His cheeks too were wet with tears. Benson knew they would have heard the shooting clearly, and they would have guessed what it was. He went to the sink to wash the blood off his hands.

'Did he make Bryan watch?' his mother asked and Benson nodded. 'Sadistic bastard.'

The following day Benson set about digging a mass grave in the walled garden for the thirty dead hounds. The horses went up for sale the same day and the other hunt servants were officially informed that their services would no longer be required, but were told nothing about the slaughter. No one wanted to think about it, let alone speak of it. Benson's ears continued to ring for several weeks as he set about cleaning the kennels and converting them into a chicken house.

Three months after the slaughter of the hounds, Phyllis went to clean the bathroom in the big house, carefully knocking first to be sure that there was no one in there. The Colonel was never one for personal modesty and was known for not locking the doors of bathrooms and toilets, and for making no effort to cover himself if someone walked in on him. Quite often he would be too drunk by the time he went to bed to undress himself, or he would get as far as taking his clothes off, but not as far as pulling on any pyjamas. Lady Grace had given up remonstrating with him on the subject many years before and merely moved to a bedroom in a distant part of the house. So, it was not a complete surprise for Phyllis to be confronted by her employer's naked backside as she came into the room. Still, she let out a small, startled squeak, apologised out of habit, and backed straight out. What aroused her suspicions that something unusual was afoot was the fact that the Colonel did not shout anything obscene or suggestive after her. She paused on the landing, suddenly aware that there was a silence hanging in the air, which was extremely rare if the Colonel was anywhere in the vicinity.

She returned to the door and listened for a few more moments, then tapped discreetly.

'Is everything all right, Colonel?' she enquired, but still there was no answer.

She pushed the door open again and the scene remained unchanged. Now that she took the time to look more closely, she realised that he was kneeling on the floor and that his head was far further down the toilet than would have been the case if he was vomiting.

'Colonel?'

Still no reply, so she moved closer. There was evidence of vomit around the rim of the bowl, where his hirsute shoulders were resting. Forcing back the urge to vomit herself, she moved him to one side and he rolled onto the floor, his hair matted and wet, his eyes staring. There was no question that he was dead. Phyllis swallowed hard and wiped a sheen of sweat from her forehead as she spread a towel over him, to afford him at least a modicum of dignity, and left the room, quietly closing the door behind her. She took several deep breaths and forced herself to walk slowly as she descended the stairs.

Lady Grace was still in the breakfast room, reading the paper, when Phyllis broke the news to her. Her Ladyship received the information calmly.

'Would you mind calling the doctor, Phyllis?' she said, folding the paper and taking a final sip from her coffee cup. 'He would probably like to hear from the person who actually found the body. I believe he has to come out to confirm the cause of death, and he can see if the police want to come and check that there are no signs of foul play.'

Phyllis did as she was asked and the doctor arrived, followed half an hour later by a couple of policemen. They all spoke in hushed, reverential tones, and the doctor, who had been looking after the health of the family all his professional life, assured Lady Grace that her husband hadn't suffered, although Lady Grace gave no sign of being concerned that he might have.

'Massive heart attack would be my guess, Your Ladyship,' he said, 'wouldn't have felt a thing. Didn't even put his hand out to save himself from diving in head first.'

The post-mortem confirmed the doctor's guesswork and the funeral was held in the village church a couple of weeks later. Every seat was taken, with more villagers standing outside to witness the coffin being carried in for the service, and out again to be buried next to his parents and grandparents. Some people muttered phrases such as 'We won't see his like again' and 'They don't make them like that anymore', and 'It's the end of an era'. Many others remained silent, apparently lost in their own private memories of the man who had more or less ruled the village for nearly half a century.

Bryan and Benson were both pall-bearers and neither of them showed even a flicker of emotion. In fact, there was not a wet eye in the whole church. The vicar talked a great deal about the contribution that the Colonel and his ancestors had made to the village. He mentioned his 'distinguished military career' and the 'wonderful legacy' he was leaving behind him, in the form of beautiful gardens and a perfectly preserved village. No one else spoke. They sang some hymns; they said some prayers and then those who considered Lady Grace to be a friend went back to the house for the tea and sandwiches that Phyllis and her mother had helped the cook to prepare. A number of people commented over the following days that Lady Grace had seemed to be on particularly good form at the tea.

CHAPTER SEVENTEEN

Once Daisy and Molly had disappeared through the garden wall, clutching the suitcase and the bleeding Trotsky, Benson waited a few minutes before plodding back to the house, this time with his wheelbarrow, as Mrs Woodcock had requested. By the time he arrived, she had already made a start on bringing the books down from the top floor and was piling them outside the French windows.

'You want me to burn the lot?' Benson asked as he filled the first barrow load.

'I don't care what you do with them,' she snapped, 'as long as they're out of my sight. You two cluttered the whole house up with all your nonsense. I need the space in the bedrooms. The builders need to get in there.'

'They're just stories,' he protested, and for a second, she saw a glimpse of Little Tom from sixty years earlier, the quiet little boy who would trail behind her obediently, only occasionally daring to speak up in contradiction to one of her bossy instructions. His hair always needed trimming, even then, a heavy fringe falling down over his eyes so that he developed a habit of jutting out his lower jaw and puffing upwards to clear it away, and his hands always needed washing, as they still did. Every detail of the day when things changed was engraved on her memory, and in her heart. She had been looking for him everywhere that afternoon, wanting him to go down to the lake with her, to help her push the boat out so that they could play 'Swallows and Amazons', secretly hopeful that she would bump into Bryan by chance as she searched the house and grounds. Just being bathed in the glow of a passing smile, or teased with a passing comment, which she would replay on an endless loop in her head, was always enough to make her day sing.

She only saw the two of them a few seconds before they saw her, but still the image of them sitting together in the folly by the lake was burned into her memory, like a red-hot branding iron sizzling into the flanks of a cow. They both looked so contented in one another's company, deep in conversation, a pile of books beside them, Bryan's arm around the boy's skinny shoulders, so that he nestled into his friend's chest, looking up like a scrappy baby bird, hoping for nourishment. She had never seen Little Tom looking that relaxed in the company of his father, or even in her company. As she watched Bryan push the boy's fringe out of his eyes with gentle affection, and heard them both laugh, she thought her heart was actually breaking in half.

'Hello, Phil,' Bryan called out when he saw her hovering at the edge of the lawn, 'come and join us.'

She would rather have run away and hidden from the sight of them being so happy without her. She could see from Little Tom's expression that he would have liked her to disappear as well. That was the moment when she knew he would no longer obey her without question. In that instant she felt like an outsider in the tiny group of people that mattered more to her than anyone else in the world. But she didn't run, because if she had then there would have been no chance of returning with any dignity at all. So, she walked over to them, trying to smile, trying to look like it didn't feel like there was a dagger lodged in her chest.

'I was just telling Tom about Dr Syn,' Bryan said, holding up the paperback, showing her the cover. 'Have you read the books? He's this vicar who is secretly the leader of a gang of smugglers, known to his followers only as "the Scarecrow". I think he would like them, don't you?'

'Why do you like books so much?' she asked, struggling not to pout as she sat on the other side of him, leaning against him, desperate to be closer to him than Little Tom was, horribly aware that she wasn't, fearful that she was forcing herself on them, that they didn't want her there. Determined not to leave, or cry. Praying that something would change but knowing that it wasn't going to.

'So many reasons,' he said, putting his other arm round her shoulders and giving her a reassuring squeeze, as if he instinctively understood how excluded she was feeling. 'To start with, they are an escape into another world.'

'I like this world,' she told him. 'Don't you?'

'Not always. You are a lucky girl to be so contented with the life you have.'

Those words told her that he didn't understand how she was feeling at all. He had no idea of the yearning churning she felt inside whenever she thought about him, or saw him, or heard his voice. She was very sure that there was nothing to be found in any book that could soothe those feelings away. She was destined to live with them forever. And now she could see that he liked Little Tom better than he liked her, just because they both liked to read books. It felt like an impossibly wide chasm was yawning up between them.

Sixty years later she could finally rid herself of the piles of books, which had reminded her of that day every time she saw them. Even once she had banished them to the room at the end of the top floor, once Bryan was unaware of anything happening beyond his bedroom door, she still knew they were there, bearing down on her spirits from on high, reminding her that she could never be his first love.

Benson pushed the wheelbarrow slowly back to his cottage, surprised by just how heavy it was, reminded that he was no longer as strong as he had once been, remembering how strong his father had been until the day the stroke arrived and he was rendered helpless forever more. One moment he had been able to lift whole tree stumps unaided, the next he was unable to even lift his own arm. He pushed the thought to the back of his mind as he carried the books inside, stacking them randomly on and around his kitchen table, before heading back for another load. He intended to have a careful look through them before deciding which ones he wanted to re-read, or maybe just keep because of the memories that the covers rekindled of a time before Bryan was removed from his life.

CHAPTER EIGHTEEN

Mrs Woodcock poked a suspicious finger at the pink phone Zahara had given her. She had been reluctant to accept the gift at first, but Zahara had insisted, and had even given her some lessons in how to log on to her various platforms, so that she could follow what was happening with the wedding arrangements online. She had tried to protest that she wanted nothing to do with modern technology, that the old landline to the house was more than enough for her needs, but Zahara had seemed not to hear her. To get her message across to the headstrong young woman, she would have had to shout in an unseemly way, so it was easier just to pretend she was listening to what she was being told. To her surprise, once she overcame her initial fear of breaking the phone, or of suddenly accessing something she had no wish to see, she was finding it hard to resist returning to Zahara's sites every hour or two in order to check if anything new had been uploaded from some other corner of the rapidly transforming estate that surrounded her cottage. She wouldn't normally have been able to spare so much time for such a frivolous pastime, but since the big house was now flooded with people doing the jobs that she would normally have had to do herself, and a lot more, it didn't seem unreasonable to indulge herself in a few hours of internet exploration each day. She wondered if she was becoming addicted, but decided she didn't care. Fewer and fewer things seemed to hold any importance for her now that Bryan had gone, taking with him all her daily responsibilities. Watching her world reduced to a small screen and being taken over by so many young people, all of whom were entirely unknown to her, left her feeling empty, but that emptiness was a surprisingly comfortable feeling, similar to the feelings she would get from the successful completion of a cleaning task, so she kept giving in to the temptation to watch more and think less about the things that had once obsessed her during her waking hours, and sometimes even in her dreams.

Swept along by Zahara's overwhelming enthusiasm for the whole event, and her Mama's obvious pride in her daughter, and even, perhaps, in her future daughter-in-law, Mrs Woodcock was finding herself troubled by mixed and confusing emotions as the wedding arrangements built up. It made her remember the joy she took as a child, imagining in the privacy of her bedroom how she would one day marry Bryan, kissing her pillow in an ecstasy of happiness as she pictured him promising to cherish her for as long as they both should live. She had often persuaded Little Tom to sneak into the village church with her, hiding at the back, during wedding ceremonies, just so she could witness the moments when the brides and grooms were united in front of the altar. She would hold tight onto Little Tom's hand, refusing to let him wriggle free in his attempts to escape the boredom of being forced to be indoors. Even the distant memory of those moments still made her heart flutter a little. And then she remembered the humiliation of the night she was summoned to the big house, when she was sixteen years old.

Her mother came back to the cottage from the kitchen, where she had been clearing up after the family's dinner, and shook her awake.

'They want to see you, Philly,' she said, 'in the drawing room.'

'See me? Why?' she asked, as she fumbled to pull her clothes on and pin up her sleep-tangled hair. 'Have I done something wrong?'

Her first thought was that Lady Grace had found out what the Colonel had done to her that day in his study, and was going to accuse her of leading her husband astray. Maybe she was going to be sent away, to remove whatever temptation she was causing.

'Don't worry,' her mother tried to reassure her, but didn't seem able to look her in the eye as she hurried her out of the cottage. 'I will be just outside the door.'

Neither of them spoke again as they ran across the lawns to the big house, and in through the kitchens, which were still steamy from the cooking and washing up. Her mother tapped politely on the polished oak of the thick drawing-room door, through which Philly could hear a raised voice.

'Come!' the Colonel barked and Philly felt her mother propelling her forward, and heard her closing the door behind her. The room was dimly lit, mostly by the flames from the fireplace that the Colonel was standing in front of, legs akimbo, face reddened by the heat, or the whisky, or possibly just his own apparent anger. 'Ah.' He tried to lighten his tone, to little effect. 'The lovely young Philly. Pretty as a picture, don't you think, Bryan?'

'Donald …' Philly noticed the Colonel's wife for the first time, poised on one of the sofas, a teacup resting on her knee and a glazed look in her eyes, as if trying to will herself to be somewhere other than this room. 'Don't embarrass the poor girl.'

'Nonsense, Grace, beauty should be given its due. The girl doesn't get enough compliments, shut away in this backwater.'

Bryan was sitting at the other end of the sofa from his mother, his eyes cast down to the floor. Despite being in his mid-thirties, he looked like a small boy, shy in the presence of adults.

'Look at her, Bryan, for God's sake, she's an absolute cracker, living right under your nose here, and you hardly seem to have noticed. Look at her!'

Bryan obeyed his father, and gave Philly a reassuring smile, but she could see his eyes were glistening with tears of humiliation and she quickly averted her own gaze back down to the thick Turkish rug. She didn't want to make him feel any worse by showing him her own pain. She hated the Colonel for his cruelty towards his son, even more than she hated him for what he had done to her.

'Stand up, boy!' the Colonel roared, suddenly infuriated by his son's gentle presence in the room, by his very existence. 'A lady has entered the room. Give her a peck on the cheek at least.'

Bryan opened his mouth to protest, but his mother reached over and placed a warning hand on his knee. She was the most skilled of all of them in handling the Colonel when he was drunk beyond reason. Her method was simply to offer no resistance and get out of his way as soon as possible. She knew that in the morning he would be an entirely different person, and would probably remember nothing of the previous evening.

Grace mouthed something to her son and he rose from his seat, walked across the room and put his arms around Philly. He smelled so good, like he had bathed before changing for dinner. She leant against him and felt the warmth of his body.

'I'm so sorry,' he whispered into her ear, his face so close she was sure she felt the featherlight touch of his lips. 'He's drunk.'

'You have to marry him, Philly,' the Colonel boomed, seemingly thrilled at the apparent success of his matchmaking skills. 'He's not much of a catch, I'll grant you that, but you would then be mistress of the house once we've gone. What do you say to that?'

'Donald!' Grace spoke more firmly this time. 'Philly, take no notice of him. I'm so sorry you have been dragged out of your bed for this. You should go back home now.'

Philly was grateful to be allowed to escape the family tension, but despite the humiliation, she wasn't sorry that it had happened. She would never forget what it felt like to have him put his arms around her so protectively, and to feel his breath on her ear, his lips brushing her cheek. As soon as she was outside the room, her mother hurried her back to bed. She didn't say a word, but she seemed to Philly to be physically trembling with suppressed fury.

The following morning Lady Grace came to the cottage with a bunch of flowers for her, selected personally from the cutting beds, and apologised again for her husband's behaviour.

'Please don't blame Bryan,' she said, 'he values your friendship enormously and he would be heartbroken to lose it.'

Philly had not known what to say, so she accepted the flowers politely and never spoke of the incident again, although no day passed without her imagining what it would be like if Bryan decided to follow his father's advice after all, and most of her nights contained dreams of those few tense moments in his arms, like the time he had comforted her after she was assaulted and the moments when he had held her in the swimming pool.

CHAPTER NINETEEN

Mrs Woodcock was standing at the sink in the cottage that her family had lived in for generations, staring out the window towards the big house, which was literally gleaming in the morning light from all the attention that was being lavished upon it. It looked like it could have been built that day, the brickwork was so clean, centuries of dirt having been blasted away by teams of craftsmen. The cottage seemed dark by contrast. It needed cleaning from top to bottom, but she didn't feel ready to tackle the task. It had the musty smell of unused and unheated rooms. For the last few years of Bryan's life she had hardly been there, wanting always to be close by in the big house in case he needed her, snatching a few hours' sleep each night in the room off the kitchen, once she had managed to get him settled till the morning, joined to him at all times by a bedside bell.

The cottage that had seemed such a warm, safe, comfortable home all her life now seemed small and cramped and unloved. Looking after the big house had taken every minute of every day, leaving her no time to think or remember what life had been like when her mother and father were still alive. Now they were gone and forgotten and there was an army of people swarming through every room and there was no reason for her to be there, nothing to distract her from the thoughts that Daisy had planted in her head.

Spotting Benson and his dog passing with a wheelbarrow, she tapped on the window. He paused, waiting as she struggled to force it open, the dog sitting obediently at his feet, head cocked in expectation.

'I'm just putting the kettle on,' she said, 'do you want a cup of tea?'

Benson looked surprised, followed by suspicious. 'A cup of tea?' he repeated, checking that he had heard right.

'Come inside and take the weight off your feet,' she said and went to open the door for him.

He paused for a moment on the doorstep, waiting for her to tell him to take off his boots, but she said nothing, so he did it anyway.

'Sit yourself down,' she said, indicating the kitchen table. 'Sorry about the state of the place. I need to give it a thorough going over.'

'Been a few years since I was in here,' he said, looking around, 'had a few good teas off your mum at this table.'

Mrs Woodcock smiled at the distant memory of her mother's chocolate brownies and Victoria sponges, and for a moment Benson saw a flash of the child in her, his best friend throughout his early years, until Bryan introduced him to the alternative universes contained in books. Neither spoke until they were both sitting with cups and saucers in front of them. Mrs Woodcock had laid a few Rich Tea biscuits on a plate.

'So, what do you think, then?' she asked.

'About what?'

'About what she was saying.'

'The French woman?'

'Yes.'

'Stuff and nonsense.' He relit his cigarette and she let the rebellious gesture pass, putting it down to him feeling nervous about facing up to the subject she was raising.

'Would be good to know once and for all.'

'Would it? I wouldn't want that man for a father.'

'It would make us brother and sister.'

'It's bad enough that we're cousins,' he grunted, more out of habit than actual distaste. She chose to ignore him, taking a sip of her tea.

'But it would be nice to know if Bryan was our brother.'

'What if it turned out to be true for one of us but not the other,' Benson asked, after a few moments' thought.

'It would still be good to know, don't you think? To know for sure.'

'Some things are best left as they are, if you ask me.'

'I loved him so much,' she said. 'So did you.'

Benson said nothing, concentrating on dunking a biscuit in his tea.

'Maybe the Colonel wasn't all bad,' he said, after a few more moments' thought.

'He did it to me,' she said, but Benson didn't react. 'He raped me.'

There was a long silence as he tried to take in the information and come up with a truthful response. 'He couldn't resist a pretty face,' he said eventually, 'that's for sure.'

Mrs Woodcock laughed, taking him by surprise. 'I suppose that is the closest I am ever going to get to a compliment from you, Tom Benson.'

'Reckon it might be,' he grinned, embarrassed to have been caught out complimenting her and relieved that she didn't expect him to dwell any deeper on the news she had just imparted. There were so many things in the past that he didn't want to think about now.

'Our mothers were both pretty when they were young,' she reminded him. 'There are photographs to prove it.'

Every year the Colonel had hired a local photographer to come to the house to take a group picture of the family and all the staff from the estate, everyone sitting in strict order of seniority on chairs that had been set out on the lawn. The fading prints had been framed and still lined the passage from the kitchen to the boot room.

'That they were,' Benson agreed. 'Their mother was a good-looking woman too, by all accounts, when she was young.'

'And neither of them had a good word to say for him, that I can remember.'

Benson nodded his agreement, relighting the stub, which had already fizzled out on his lip.

'But would either of them want us to know the truth, if that is what happened to them?' she went on. 'If they had wanted us to know, they would have told us themselves, don't you think?'

'Never talked about anything like that,' Benson said. 'Not like people do today. Some things are best left unspoken. They can't be changed now.'

'If it's true, do you think it's possible we aren't the only children he had on the other side of the blanket?'

'It's possible,' he said, without having to pause to think about it.

'We could have any number of brothers and sisters.'

'Who sired me isn't that important,' Benson said after a few moments of reflection, 'unless you are planning to show me at Crufts, or put me out to stud.'

Today was the first time he had seen her laugh since she was a child, when she had pushed him off the rowing boat into the lake after he had tried to kiss her, and the swans had chased him all the way back to the bank.

CHAPTER TWENTY

'It's only me, Gran,' Molly called out as she pushed hard against the cottage door to get past the piles of rugs.

'Oh, hello, lovey!' The old woman's face lit up at the sight of her granddaughter.

'It's dark in here, Gran.' Molly pulled back the curtains, sending a shaft of light slicing through the dust.

'Don't go letting in the draught, lovey.'

'It's all right, Gran, there's no wind today.'

'I feel the cold more, now I can't move around so much.'

Molly kissed the top of her head and the old woman extended a claw-like hand for a squeeze.

'Fancy a cup of tea, Gran?'

'Oooh, yes please. Put the kettle on for me, there's a good girl. Make mine a strong one. You come home for a visit, have you?'

'I'm doing a job, up at the big house, so I thought I'd pop in and see how you're doing.'

'At the big house? You don't want to be going up there, lovey. You want to steer clear of that man. You listen to your old Gran; she knows a thing or two.'

'I bet you do, Gran.' Molly lifted the Aga lid and set the kettle on the hot plate. 'Which man would that be then? Who should I steer clear of?'

'You know who I mean. He was the death of your grand-father, that man.'

'You mean the old Colonel? He's been dead forty years or more.'

'Has he?' Gran narrowed her eyes as if trying to bring the years into focus. 'Good riddance to bad rubbish, that's what I say.'

'His son died the other day too. Bryan Toby.'

'Young Bryan died? He was a lovely boy. So handsome. Never seen a boy so beautiful. More like a girl.'

'I think he was ninety-odd, Gran.'

'Young Bryan was ninety? I'm ninety.'

'I know you are, Gran. You're going to live forever.' The kettle belched steam as Molly rinsed out two tea-stained mugs. 'How did the old Colonel kill Grandad, then?'

'Worked him to death. Worked him to death on the farm, then sold it out from under him and worked him to death behind the bar in that pub. And that wasn't the half of it.'

'I thought you liked working behind the bar.'

'I did, whenever that man wasn't hanging around, making a pest of himself. But your grandad had a weak heart. It was too much, lugging those barrels around. He should have been allowed to retire. He should have been given a decent pension. He made a lot of money for that family over the years, and his father before him.'

'What was the other half then?' Molly filled the mugs and stirred the tea bags to strengthen the brew.

'The other half of what, lovey?'

'What else did the Colonel do to Grandad?'

'I could tell you some stories.'

Molly popped the mug down beside her grandmother. 'There's your tea, Gran. What stories?'

'Bless you. They're not stories for young ears.'

'I'm a grown-up now, Gran.'

'So you are, lovey.' She peered closely at her granddaughter. 'What are you doing back in the village?'

'I'm helping organise a wedding up at the big house.'

'Who's getting married then?'

'A friend of mine.'

'That was a beautiful house once, built on the backs of people like us. You should have seen the gardens. They were a picture. Make sure they treat you right, lovey. A pretty girl like you can get into a lot of trouble up there. I was pretty once.' She gestured towards a framed photograph on the mantel above the Aga.

'You've always been beautiful, Gran.'

'Pah. For all the good it did me. Men like that think they can take whatever they want.'

'Men like the Colonel?'

'You steer clear of him.'

'He's dead, Gran.'

'Good riddance! What about you? You got a nice young man?'

'Nah, Gran. I'm fine on my own.'

The old woman nodded, staring at her granddaughter, apparently lost in thought, but possibly just lost.

'We found some old articles about Bryan Toby and his friends being arrested up at the house,' Molly said. 'Do you remember that happening?'

'I remember reading about it in the papers. It was a crying shame what they did to that boy. It was his father who should have been locked up, not him. He came sniffing round here when your grandfather was out in the fields. There was no stopping him. Girls in your generation wouldn't put up with it, I can tell you, and good for you. But we didn't know, my generation. We didn't know.'

'The Colonel made a pass at you?'

'He took advantage of his position, but I made him pay for it in the end, that's all I'm going to say on the subject. I will say one other thing though. No matter what you find out, Molly, your grandfather will always be your grandfather. He was a good man and he would have been proud to have a granddaughter like you.' She dabbed at her nose with the tissue she kept permanently screwed up in her hand. 'There's some biscuits in that tin.'

'Mum says there was a trust fund set up for my education,' Molly said as she fetched the tin. 'Was that your doing? Is that how you made him pay?'

'You don't need to worry your young head about any of that,' Alice said, snapping off a piece of biscuit with shaky fingers, spraying crumbs into her lap.

'Do you remember a young French girl working up at the house, after the war?' Molly asked. 'She was a groom, I think. Claudette.'

'Claudette?' The old woman repeated the name and seemed to become lost once more in her own memories as Molly passed her another biscuit. 'Why would you ask about Claudette?'

'Her daughter is staying at the pub.'

'She has a little girl?'

'Not that little, Gran, she's in her seventies.'

Her grandmother chewed thoughtfully on a shard of biscuit. 'Yes,' she said eventually, 'I suppose she would be now.'

'So, you remember her?'

'Remember who, lovey?'

'Claudette.'

'The less said about that palaver the better. You come home for a visit, have you?'

CHAPTER TWENTY-ONE

The unexpected roar of the helicopter drowned the sound of the horses' hooves in the high street as they danced nervously backwards, and set dogs barking in the surrounding houses, while the wind from the rotor blades forced the newly planted trees on the estate to bow low as Vijay approached. Zahara was filming over her father's shoulder as he brought them down to land on the newly laid turf, which had arrived a few weeks earlier, rolled up like gigantic green carpets on the backs of several lorries. Charu, Vijay's lawyer and closest business confidante, was strapped in beside her, so close Zahara could smell her perfume, but she did not turn the camera in her direction. Mama, who had flatly refused to fly with them, had been driven down earlier and was already waiting on the steps of the house. She had said she didn't want to fly because she didn't trust her husband's piloting skills, but Zahara was pretty sure it was because she didn't want to be in a confined space with Charu. It was not, however, a subject either of them would ever speak about out loud. Most of the time, Zahara managed not to think about it at all.

'This is my dad, everyone,' Zahara told her followers as she ran behind Vijay across the lawn. 'He's come to see how we are getting on with the renovations.' She caught up with him. 'What do you think of the place, Daddy?'

'Very beautiful, baby. I can see why you love it. But we can make it even more beautiful for you.' He did not slow his pace as he turned to the camera, arms stretched wide, jogging backwards as he declaimed to the world, 'This will be the most beautiful fairy-tale wedding the world has ever seen. It's like we have travelled back in time. It's like the British Empire never died. My little princess will be a queen, an empress, in her palace.'

As he ran into the house, laughing gleefully at everything that he had the power and money to do, he greeted the workmen like long-lost friends as they shrank back out of his way on the stairs. Nothing could be allowed to impede the speed of his progress through his days. There were not enough hours in the universe to allow for delays. Charu followed, a few steps behind, cooler, calmer, but just as fast, her eyes and thumbs on her phone, but still managing to avoid the obstacle course of wet paint and missing floorboards laid by the army of electricians and decorators still at work. Zahara was just behind, swinging her camera around the chaos and jabbering excitedly to her followers about the fabulous work the decorators were doing. Mama started to follow them across the hallway, but they were already almost at the top of the stairs when she decided to pause and take a deep gasp of breath. Only then did she notice Mrs Woodcock, on a visit from the cottage, standing in the door to the kitchen area, watching the arrival.

'Would you like a cup of tea?' Mrs Woodcock asked and Mama nodded, meekly following the housekeeper as she led her into the service area of the house, away from the clamour and glamour of the grand rooms. As the door clicked shut behind her, the frenetic sounds of full-scale renovation faded to a dull and distant hum.

. . .

Daisy was surprised to see Gerald's number coming up on her phone as she strolled through the village with Trotsky, returning the waves and greetings of locals who had come to think of her as a permanent fixture in the pub, even though few of them had exchanged more than a passing greeting with her. The strolls had become her morning routine. She had come to feel quite at home amongst the people she saw most evenings in the pub, able to greet many of them by name, although now the weather was growing colder, she was missing the warm Mediterranean breezes.

'Hello, Gerald.'

'Good morning. I'm sorry to disturb you. Are you still in the village?'

'I thought I would stay for a little while. I want to find out more about my father. It has been very pleasant here, but now I think the weather is changing.'

'I thought I should just warn you that there is something happening that I can't quite understand.' Gerald sounded tired. 'A company in Singapore has taken over the estate's debt. It is one of those impenetrable property-development-based conglomerates, which mainly seems to exist to reduce tax bills in other countries. It is behind many of the tallest tower blocks in Dubai, and hotels and golf courses everywhere. It seems a little …' He paused, searching for the right word. 'I wouldn't say exactly "sinister", but definitely opaque.'

'What about the plan for a caravan park?'

'Apparently, there have been a number of new plans hatched since then, none of them particularly realistic. A lot of people have dreamed big dreams, or perhaps I should say fantasies, around that house. Property developers do tend to blow with the political winds. But now there has been some sort of deal struck, behind closed doors, between a couple of big international players in the market. I can't enlighten you any more than that, I'm afraid. I feel that I am rather out of my depth now that I am out of touch most days, so I have involved a young associate of mine in Zurich. Would you like me to send you his name and number, just in case you need any assistance? He understands these things much better than I do. He has his finger more on the pulse of things.'

'Okay, thank you. Have you passed any of this information to Mr Benson and Mrs Woodcock?'

'I haven't. At our meeting I was left with the distinct impression that they really did not want to be bothered with any of it. I think that Bryan took very good care of them in many ways, just as they took care of him in so many other ways. I don't think he burdened them with any of the financial problems of the estate, and now they do not seem able to take in what is happening.'

'Like children who have never had to grow up or take responsibility for their own lives?'

'Yes.' He seemed to be thinking her words through. 'That is probably a good description of their state of mind. Some might say they have been institutionalised, like soldiers who do not know what to do with their days when they leave the army and have no one to issue them with instructions. I feel that I should be looking after their interests, much as I looked after Bryan's, but I fear I am not up to the challenge.'

'Are you well, Gerald?' Daisy asked. 'You do not sound like your usual self.'

'Just feeling my age, my dear, but thank you for asking. I find the modern world has become very exhausting. Everything is so much more complicated than it used to be. I pine for simpler times.'

• • •

The kitchen in the big house was warm, and infused with the comforting scents of the tens of thousands of meals that had been cooked within its walls through the centuries. Neither Zahara's Mama nor Mrs Woodcock felt the need to speak until the tea had been poured and they were both seated at the kitchen table, on well-worn wooden chairs.

'Lady Grace used to come in here a lot when I was a child,' Mrs Woodcock said, 'just sitting where you are, having a cup of tea and chatting with my mother.'

'Lady Grace?' Mama was unsure why she had followed the housekeeper into her shabby realm, or why she felt so close to tears. She released her dog onto the floor, where it sat, quivering, staring up at her, unable to work out what was expected of it. 'Who is Lady Grace?'

'Oh, she's long gone now. She was the lady of the house here when I was young. She's the one in the portrait upstairs, on a horse, surrounded by hounds. She was very beautiful. A real lady of the old school. Never a hair out of place. She and my mother got on well. My mother was a baby when Lady Grace and the Colonel married, and she became the housekeeper when she was thirty, when her mother, my grandmother, died. My mother was a good listener. I think coming in here was like a refuge for Her Ladyship sometimes. My mother was born on the estate, in the same cottage I was born in. She started as a parlour maid when she was fourteen and worked her way up, so she knew the house better than Lady Grace did. There was nothing went on here that my mother didn't know about, although she would never gossip about anything to do with the house or family. Her Ladyship knew that. She appreciated it. The Colonel was not a kind man, although he managed to make himself popular enough in some quarters of the village.'

'My husband is also a very popular man,' Mama surprised herself with her own words, 'in many parts of the world. But then he has a lot of money and people find that very attractive. Many women seem to find him irresistible.' She dabbed the corners of her heavily mascaraed eyes and her dog let out an almost indiscernible whimper of distress.

'The Colonel looked good in pictures, but he was not an attractive man, because of his nasty nature,' Mrs Woodcock continued, enjoying the novelty of talking frankly about things she had always instinctively believed were not supposed to be spoken about. 'But he was very forceful. I think perhaps some women found that attractive, or at least gave him the impression that they did. After the Colonel died, Her Ladyship spent less and less time here and more time at their flat in London, or travelling to the south of France. I think perhaps she was trying to escape bad memories.'

'Do you know,' Mama appeared to have stopped listening, having drifted away with her own preoccupations, 'on the day that my daughter, Zahara, was born, one of my father-in-law's servants also gave birth. It was only many years later that I discovered that my husband was also the father of that child. On the same day! And now I hear that he is a grandfather, several times over. People in the family talk about it openly, if they think I am not listening. But I am always listening. I can't help hearing. Half my family disapproves of the way Zahara has chosen to lead her life, but they will still come to the wedding and eat our food, because Vijay tells them to, and everyone wants to please Vijay. They say they feel sorry for me because they don't believe Zahara will ever give me grandchildren, but they don't really care about how I feel. It is just an entertaining story for people to tell one another. It has become part of the legend of Vijay. What can we do? It is the way that men are.'

'There are some good men,' Mrs Woodcock said, remembering Bryan's angelic smile, and the scent of his skin when he had been lying in the sun.

Mama shook her bracelets down her arms and lifted her teacup for a sip. 'My father was just the same. Perhaps that is why I agreed to marry Vijay. It was what I was used to.'

'Your father was a man of power also?'

'Oh yes. He and his father built a great fortune. Just like Vijay and his father and grandfather. That is why they wanted us to marry, to amalgamate the fortunes. Both our families became rich by supplying the British Empire with everything they needed while they were in India. They supplied the Army and the civil servants. Whatever the British needed, my family would find it for them, from army uniforms to railway sleepers, food, bricks, motor cars, tyres, whatever they needed. Now everything is in Vijay's hands and he has made it even bigger. Property, property everywhere. Huge skyscrapers. Huge developments. Huge deals. All over the world. My father had unlimited energy, just like Vijay. He had many mistresses too. My mother also had to put up with it.'

'Did those mistresses bear him children?' Mrs Woodcock asked, after a long pause.

Mama looked momentarily surprised by such a direct question, then shrugged. 'I don't know.'

'Would you like to know? Would you like to meet your half-brothers and half-sisters, if they exist?'

'That is a strange question to ask.' Mama looked for a moment as if she was going to remind Mrs Woodcock of her position, but then gave an involuntary shiver, and dabbed again at the corners of her eyeliner. 'I have thought about it more often in recent years. I have wondered what I would say to Zahara if she said she wanted to meet whatever half-siblings her father has produced.'

'And what have you decided?'

'I have decided nothing.'

• • •

Gerald had sent through a name, Robert Duvalier, and a Zurich number. Daisy googled and found pictures of a smoothly dressed young corporate lawyer standing amidst other smoothly dressed men from the world of global finance and politics, some in the flowing white robes of the Gulf States, most in dark-blue suits, white shirts and slim, bright ties, all standing in lines, or shaking hands with one another, smiling into the cameras. There were several professional profiles, listing his educational achievements and dry records of employment in a variety of law firms around the world. She sent a message, using Gerald's name as an introduction.

The reply, 'How can I help?', was almost instant. It seemed Gerald's name still held some power in the legal world. Daisy gave him the name of the Toby family estate and asked if he had any idea who now owned the debt. There was a pause, she presumed while he did some research. 'There has been a flurry of interest surrounding this property in the last few months,' was the next message. 'It seems to have been added to the portfolio of a holding company based partly in Singapore and partly in Dubai.'

'Does the holding company have interests in property development?' Daisy asked.

'It seems to mainly be hospitality, amongst many other things. A large number of hotels. It is just one part of a larger operation, which seems to be built on an international property portfolio. There are a lot of building companies under the same umbrella.'

'I plan to be in Zurich soon,' Daisy wrote. 'I would very much like to take you to lunch.'

• • •

Molly had come across her mother clearing out the flower beds around the pub's terrace, preparing them for winter. The sun had come out, making the afternoon surprisingly warm. She picked up a rake to help.

'I went to see Gran this morning,' she said.

'Yes.' Joan didn't look up from her labours. 'She told me. She seemed pretty clear-headed about the whole visit. Some days she's as sharp as a tack. It seems you managed to trigger a lot of memories for her.'

'When you were a child here,' Molly continued in the same casual tone, 'did the squire from the big house come in to drink much?'

'The Colonel?' Joan straightened up and massaged her back as she delved into her memory, deciding which snippets to share with her daughter. 'Yes. He was here a lot. It was a bit of a joke amongst the others that he had a soft spot for your grandmother. He was famous for being a bit gropey after a few whiskies.'

'Did Grandad not mind?'

'He didn't like it, but then he didn't like the man anyway. But publicans have to get used to dealing with drunks behaving inappropriately. People do and say all sorts of stupid things when they've had a few. Well, you know that as well as I do. Why all the questions?'

'When I told Gran I was working up at the big house, she got quite agitated. Told me I should steer clear of "that man". She seemed to think he was still alive.'

'She must have had a sleep between you going and me arriving,' Joan said. 'She didn't say anything weird to me.'

'She kept saying how bad he was.'

'He was always very nice to me, pressing money into my hand if I ever brought him a drink. After he'd had a few, he would get a bit tactile, cuddling me and telling me that I was going to "grow up to be a beauty", that sort of thing, which was a bit uncomfortable. But you have to put up with that sort of thing from time to time in this trade.'

'Do you, though?'

'You know what it's like; we had to prise a few customers off you in your teen years.'

'Yes—' Molly gave a theatrical shiver at the memory '—and you think we have to put up with that sort of thing, just because we work in a pub?'

'Wow, you're in a feisty mood today.'

'Me? Feisty? I wonder where I get that from?' Molly wasn't smiling, so Joan decided not to engage any further, to avoid the conversation escalating into a row, and went back to working with the rake.

Neither of them noticed the open window a few feet above them, where Daisy was taking an afternoon rest on her bed as their conversation floated up through the peaceful afternoon air.

CHAPTER TWENTY-TWO

As Bryan Toby hit the ground, he heard his old bones snapping. It would be ten more years before he died, almost to the day, but the day he tripped and fell would be the last time that Benson would ever see him. They had been sitting together all morning, as was their habit at that time, in Benson's kitchen, discussing a book, *Tom Brown's School Days*, which Benson had found in a second-hand shop while in town, waiting for the Bentley to be serviced at the garage that had been looking after the car ever since the Colonel bought it in the nineteen sixties. Both of them had now read the book and enjoyed it for differing reasons, which they had been sharing. Bryan remembered reading it before, as a child, and saw different things in it to admire now that he was old. Benson had made them their daily coffee in the coffee-pod machine that Bryan had recently instructed him to buy for exactly this purpose.

'I made the mistake of reading it before I was sent off to boarding school,' Bryan recalled. 'It frightened the life out of me. I was quite sure that I would end up being toasted over the fire by sadistic prefects like Flashman.'

'And were you?' Benson asked.

'Luckily for me, and thanks to my mother's gene pool, I was very beautiful, and a lot of the bigger boys were keen to act as my protectors,' Bryan replied. 'Reading it now makes me think a lot about my father. I don't think I realised it at the time, but now I feel there may have been something of the Flashman about him. I had a worse time of it here, with him, than I ever had from bullies at school.'

'He was a strong character.' Benson spoke cautiously.

'The older I get, Tom, the more certain I become that he was a complete shit. All through my youth he convinced me that I was the one in the wrong, that I was the one letting down the family. I was the weak link, letting him and all our previous generations down. It took me a very long time to see things differently. Prison was full of bullies like my father; men who hadn't been born with the same advantages but, like him, had decided that the laws of decency and human kindness did not apply to them. Psychopaths perhaps. Sociopaths certainly. He never had to break the law because laws were made precisely to benefit people like him. He had everything handed to him on a plate, but I truly believe that if he had been born poor, he would have ended up as some sort of a gangster boss. My mother told me, long after he was dead, and after she had downed nearly a whole bottle of rosé, that for a while he used to hang out with the Kray twins in the clubs around Soho. He found them to be exciting company. Dangerous and exciting. They were the same age as me and I think he would compare me to them, and find me very lacking in manly qualities. My mother said that the day he discovered Ronnie Kray was gay, he flew into the most terrible rage. I suppose he felt they had made a fool of him, and that he would now be tainted by association. He could hardly hope to control Ronnie Kray like he controlled me, and everyone else here in the village, could he?'

They had talked for an hour or two before Bryan pulled himself shakily to his feet and set off for his daily walk around the grounds. He never varied his route, but it took almost twice as long as it had ten years earlier. It had been raining all night and the ground was slippery. As he fell, he wished he had brought his stick with him, like Phyllis told him to every time he left the house. The nagging about the stick had become a running joke between the two of them.

Benson and Rotter, alerted that he had not returned home by a worried Mrs Woodcock, found him later in the afternoon. He was still lying where he had fallen in the mud, down by the lake, surrounded by a flock of curious swans, staying very still, soaked through from the steady drizzle that had been falling on him ever since he had slipped, waiting to be found, in far too much pain to be able to move by himself. He screamed when Benson lifted him, as easily as he might have lifted a newborn lamb on the farm, and continued screaming all the way up to the house, the terrible sound bringing Mrs Woodcock running out of the kitchen, and making Rotter circle nervously around them.

'We need to call an ambulance,' Benson said.

'No ambulance,' Bryan gasped.

'You need to go to hospital,' Benson said. 'You've obviously broken something.'

'No hospitals!' Bryan said. 'Hospitals are no better than torture chambers. Please, Tom, just carry me up to my bed.'

'Just do as you are told,' Mrs Woodcock said to him, over Bryan's head. 'I'll show you the way.'

Neither Benson nor Mrs Woodcock were comfortable with him penetrating this far into the house, but both could see this was an emergency. His father had never made it past the kitchen and her mother would have been mortified at the sight of him heading towards the bedrooms in his gardening clothes. He hadn't even taken his cap off. But then Old Benson would never have needed to come indoors, because there would have been other people working inside who would have been able to take over the heavy lifting at the door. Benson was fully conscious of how worn and dirty his clothes were in contrast with the intricate, polished furniture and lavish fabrics of the house, and wanted to retreat back outside, into his own world of vegetable beds and potting sheds, as quickly as possible.

He followed Mrs Woodcock into the master bedroom and laid the fragile old body down on the mountain of pillows that filled one end of the four-poster bed, worried that mud from his hands might brush off on the immaculately ironed white linen. Rotter looked equally ill at ease as he peered in round the bedroom door, nervously thumping his tail against the ancient oak, as if aware that he too was not supposed to be there, but too worried by the screams emanating from somewhere deep inside Bryan as they moved him, and the fear he could sense in the raised voices, to stray too far away from Benson.

'Thank you, Tom,' Bryan whispered, finally closing his eyes and sliding into a relieved slumber.

'He needs to be seen by a doctor,' Benson said as Mrs Woodcock ushered him and Rotter back down the staircase towards the door.

'We'll see what he wants to do when he wakes up,' she said. 'In the meantime, I will look after him. You need to go to a chemist and buy the strongest painkillers they will give you, for when he wakes up. A bit of TLC is all he needs to get him back on his feet. You heard what he said, loud and clear. If he doesn't want to be poked and chopped around by surgeons, then that is his decision. Leave me to sort him out. You go and make yourself useful.'

When he returned with the tablets, Mrs Woodcock informed him that Bryan was still sleeping. He came to the kitchen door many times after that, to hand over vegetables he had grown, meat he had killed, or groceries he had bought in town, and he even made it over the kitchen threshold, to eat whatever food she had prepared for the day, but he never again walked up the stairs or into the bedroom, even on the day, ten years later, when Mrs Woodcock reported that she was unable to wake Bryan up with his usual breakfast tray.

It only took a few months for being excluded from Bryan's life to feel to him like a normal state of affairs, although he never stopped missing their talks. He continued reading. In fact, he probably read more, simply to keep his mind somewhere else. To start with, he didn't think to blame her for taking his friend away. His place had always been outside in the grounds, or at home in his cottage, and that was how it would always be. Her place was inside the house, caring for

Bryan. He assumed Bryan would be back outside once his bones had knitted back together, so he resigned himself to waiting patiently.

To her, it felt like her turn had finally come. Benson could see that in her eyes. It looked like triumph and he slowly came to hate her for it. Sometimes she would even dare to venture down into the garden in order to send him on an errand in the Bentley, or to tell him to bring something from the greenhouse up to the house. It didn't seem fair that she could invade his territory, when he was banned from hers. That was when he wrote the 'bugger off' sign and stuck it on the door of the greenhouse. He needed to have at least one place that was only for him. He had been drunk when he wrote it, or he probably wouldn't have bothered, but even once he had sobered up, he never took it down. She must have sensed she was becoming unwelcome because she did not get as far as the greenhouse again until the day Gerald Remers came to see them both.

Only Bryan and Mrs Woodcock knew the private daily routines that evolved inside the master bedroom during the ten years following the fall. By the time the broken bones had mended enough to dull the pain, Bryan's muscles had lost what little strength they had still been clinging to on the day of the accident. He relied on Mrs Woodcock to get him to the bathroom to empty his bowels or to shower, or to wash him in bed when even that short walk was too much for both of them. If he needed to empty his bladder, he used bottles, which she would replace when she brought his meals, without uttering a word.

During those years she became intimate with every crevice and fold of the sagging flesh that covered his increasingly visible skeleton. She never rushed the procedures, always meticulously gentle with her fingers and with the warm, wet flannel, always keeping her gaze fixed on the job of erasing the aromas of age and decay, avoiding making any eye contact that might remind them both of who they had once been. It was more an act of piety than simply one of love. If she could have washed him only with her tears, she would have done so gladly.

To begin with, Bryan would tense up whenever she touched him, partly from the expectation of pain, partly from embarrassment at the intimacy. But, just as the pain had lessened, the self-consciousness had also relaxed with time. He learned to enjoy the sensual pleasures of their silent morning and evening rituals. He had not been intimate with anyone for forty years and the relief of feeling the loving touch of another person swept over him in an unstoppable flood, once he allowed it to be released. They never spoke of such things, both fearful that by talking about what they were feeling, they might make it impossible to continue along the same path, but both would find that sometimes their tears would spring up involuntarily while she was caring for him.

During the hours that he was alone and she was polishing the rest of the house, he would sleep or read. In a rare moment of modernisation, about ten years earlier, he had arranged for the internet to be installed throughout the estate, so sometimes he would write emails to old friends, none of whom ever suggested coming to visit him, and many of whom eventually stopped replying, perhaps because they were dead, or perhaps because he had become too much of a voice from their pasts, which they now either missed too painfully or regretted too deeply. Maybe some of them wanted to hold on to the memory of his youthful beauty, and feared what they would see if they returned to the house. Eventually, Gerald was the only one still in touch, but even then, only in writing, or the occasional, awkward phone call, during which they would talk solely about Bryan's current financial difficulties. Not that Bryan would have wanted any of the gilded youths of his past to see him in the final stages of his disintegration. If he woke in the night, he would pull out the album of photographs and gaze at the fading images of them all in their heydays, particularly himself, and let those images remain on his retinas as he drifted back to sleep. He never passed any mirrors on his increasingly rare visits to the bathroom, but he could still see the adoration in Phyllis's eyes whenever she came into the room, and that was enough.

Even as the broken bones knitted back together, other pains and difficulties took root and grew amongst his internal organs, invisible beneath the gossamer-thin skin. Each day she would ask him if he wanted her to call for professional medical help and he would shake his head, his eyes imploring her not to betray his wishes. On one day, when the struggle to get him clean very nearly defeated her, and he saw the tears streaking her cheeks, he admitted that he would rather die than go into any hospital.

'I spent time in the hospital wing of the prison,' he said. 'It was the closest thing to hell that you can imagine, Phil. I could not possibly do that again. Please don't give me back to them.'

She would never have done that, even though she knew the doctors and nurses would be kind to him in ways she could only imagine the prison staff and other inmates were not. The thought of handing his care over to others, however well-meaning they might be, was far too hard to bear. It was the first time he had ever mentioned his time in prison to her, although she was pretty sure that he had talked to Benson about it, particularly if they were discussing books that were relevant to the subject.

He slept longer and longer and more and more often, and sometimes, if it was late at night and she was confident that he wouldn't wake, she would decide not to go downstairs to the cold, narrow bed that awaited her in the scullery, but would lie down next to him, remaining quite still, listening to the rattle of his breath in the darkness, remembering how he had been when he was young. Sometimes, while she was lying beside him, his hand would twitch, his fingers would come to rest on hers and she hardly dared to breathe in case she woke him and frightened away his feather-light touch.

In the final weeks, he became restless. A pain somewhere deep inside, which he couldn't describe to her with any clarity, was increasing in intensity, and all he could do to relieve it was to moan with every intake and expulsion of air. Occasionally, he was unable to hold back a scream, which would cut through her heart, wherever she was in the house, trying to distract herself from her own emotional pain with hard work: mopping, scrubbing and polishing. The screams became more regular, until they were almost constant, but still he was able to shout 'no' when she asked if he wanted her to call for help.

She had not slept for even a moment on the night she decided to finally silence the screams and end the pain for him. Her own exhaustion helped her to decide that now was the moment. He wasn't awake; at least, he wasn't responding to the endearments she was whispering into his ear. He was lying on his back and she knew he no longer had the strength to change his position without her help, but she knelt across his chest anyway, pinning his arms down with the insides of her trembling thighs, just in case, and pressed the pillow onto his face, spreading her hands either side of his head, cupping it gently but firmly through the feathers, so that there was no chance he could turn it to the side in order to find a pocket of air that would prolong his suffering.

His body did not have the strength to struggle beneath her weight, so she could not be sure how soon he stopped breathing for good. She pressed her thighs tighter over his ribcage, trying to sense, with the most sensitive area of her body, if his heart was still beating. She couldn't feel anything other than her own pulse, but to be sure, and because she didn't want to admit that the end had finally come, she remained in the same position for at least half an hour before finally lifting the pillow and laying it to one side, stretching her body out along the full length of his, and lowering her cheek across his nose and mouth. She lay there for another half an hour, until she was certain she could feel no whisper of air, then rolled back down beside him, finally drifting into a deep, exhausted, relieved sleep.

When she woke, she went downstairs to prepare his breakfast as usual. It would sound better, she decided, if she could tell the police that she found him dead when she came in with the tray, rather than admitting she had been peacefully and knowingly sleeping, for seven blissful hours, beside his corpse.

CHAPTER TWENTY-THREE

As spring restored the havoc that had been wreaked on the garden and grounds through the autumn and winter, the iceberg roses budded with a promise of beauty to come. The lawns had healed and the pollarded trees were sprouting with a renewed green vigour. The labours of the builders and decorators inside the house were also coming to fruition in a dramatic transformation. State-of-the-art bathrooms shone in every bedroom, rotted window frames had been repaired, fresh paintwork had been applied and subtle lighting systems installed. Only the kitchen areas remained in the state they had been on the day Bryan Toby died. They now stood in a markedly shabby contrast to the rest of the gleaming house, and Mrs Woodcock found some comfort in that. Other people now used them to make tea and coffee for the workers, and to provide fridge space for those who had brought their own lunches with them. She had taken to feeding herself in her cottage and crossed the gardens to the big house less and less often. Likewise, Benson had retreated into his cottage, tending only sporadically to the small patch of garden around it, with the dog never more than a few feet away from him. He had started to re-read every book that Bryan had ever introduced him to. That was where Daisy found him on her return to the village, sitting in a deckchair that he had rescued from one of the builders' skips after they cleared out the cricket pavilion in order to convert it into a bar area.

'You?' he grunted when he eventually looked up from his book. 'Thought you'd gone back to France.'

'Yes,' she said. 'I did. I have been to other places too.'

'But you've come back.'

'Back to my roots.'

Benson gave a contemptuous snort, which made her smile.

'Not as firmly rooted as you and Madame Woodcock, perhaps, Mr Benson, but still the closest thing I have to an ancestral home. May I talk to you inside for a moment?'

It looked for a second as if he was going to say 'no', but if he was, he thought better of it and struggled out of the deckchair to lead the way into the kitchen. Bryan seemed thrilled to have a visitor in the house.

'I have been to Zurich to visit a young lawyer called Robert,' Daisy said, sitting down at the table, 'to try to find out what is happening to the estate financially.'

'Why would you do that?' Benson asked, genuinely puzzled. He had been managing to put all thoughts of the precarious future facing the house out of his mind. Such things had never been the business of anyone but Bryan and, before him, the Colonel. He actually had no idea how to even start influencing what might happen to his home next, and he had learned how to be content with that situation. Ignoring it allowed him to sleep soundly at night, and to read or garden during the day with a clear mind.

'Well, partly because I have become interested in the story of my father's family,' she said, 'and partly because I have a lot of time on my hands, and I enjoy skiing. But also, because I am worried about what might happen to you and Madame Woodcock. My brother and sister.'

Benson lit a cigarette butt from an ashtray that he had fashioned out of a foil pie dish many years before. He did not bother to contradict her.

'So, what's the story then?'

'It seems that Bryan, our brother—' she paused and waited for a reaction, but received nothing '—basically sold or mortgaged everything that was left of the estate in order to have enough money to stay here till he died. There's nothing left. No money whatsoever. The place now belongs to a company in Singapore.' She paused again, but there was still no reaction. 'The company in Singapore is not transparent in its dealings. It's almost impossible to find out information about it. It seems, however, as if the man behind it is from India, and is the father of the bride.' She waved in the direction of the house.

That elicited a raised eyebrow and a relighting of the smouldering stub, but still he said nothing. Daisy studied him with unashamed intensity, trying to imagine what it would have been like to have known him when he was a boy, before he acquired the many layers of grime, the patches of rough stubble and the lank, thinning hair. There had been many things to enjoy in her peripatetic childhood, but it might have been nice to have spent at least one summer playing on the lake with Little Tom and Philly, being allowed to run feral in the woods, maybe even squabbling like siblings always did, or so she had heard. It would have been good to have at least met Bryan. She pulled herself back into the present. There was no point dwelling on the past and what might have been. It would be better to try to shape the future for all the family. She felt a responsibility to take care of the pair of them. She didn't know who was actually the eldest amongst them, but she felt like she was their big sister because of their apparent innocence regarding the uncaring ways of the outside world that awaited them once the estate, which had nurtured them all their lives, had been taken away from them. However much they might pretend not to care, she couldn't believe that they were not frightened of the uncertainties that lay ahead.

She eventually broke the silence. 'All the renovations to the house are actually preparations for turning it into a luxury hotel once the wedding is over. They are investments for him, part of a business project.' She gave a shrug. 'I doubt even his wife or daughter know the full extent of his plans.'

'Where would that leave Phyllis and me, then?' Benson asked eventually.

'The cottages are all part of the estate, so he owns them too. I would imagine he would like to get you both out eventually, but I doubt he would legally be able to force you, since you have been living here all your lives. But there are many ways that they could make your lives very uncomfortable, and I am sure they would be willing to do that if they thought it was in their financial interests. These are people for whom profits trump all other considerations.'

Benson seemed to have stopped listening, concentrating instead on scratching Bryan behind his ears. Daisy waited for a while, to see if he was going to say anything else, but when he picked up the book lying nearest to him, *Little Lord Fauntleroy*, and started reading, she realised that he wanted to be on his own, and she reluctantly let herself out. She would leave him to think things over, she decided, and come back to try again later.

. . .

'I've got something huge to ask you,' Zahara said.

'Sure.' Molly grinned, aware that every time Zahara added something new to her wedding wish-list, it meant another mark-up for her. 'Fire away.'

'Would you be my maid of honour?'

Molly opened her mouth, but nothing came out. The camera was running, so there was no possibility she could refuse in front of millions of followers. There was no point protesting that she was hardly even a friend in the true sense, or that she knew none of the bridesmaids who had all been recruited for their beauty and dancing skills. They had been rehearsing their dances for weeks by then, and Molly had no idea how to catch up. She was also supposed to be running the wedding for Zahara as her client, which would be doubly hard if she was expected to perform maid-of-honour duties at the same time.

'That is so flattering,' she managed to squeak eventually, and Zahara clapped ecstatically, before turning off the camera.

'There is one thing you should know,' Molly said. 'I dance like a baby elephant. I have no sense of rhythm at all.'

'Oh, don't worry about that.' Zahara enveloped her in a hug, jumping up and down with excitement. 'The bridesmaids can do all that traditional stuff. I just want you by my side the whole time, plus I want you in the photographs, because you are so gorgeous! I can't wait to see you with some make-up on.'

'You two sound like you are having a good time,' Carolyn said, coming in from a run, which had left her tanned, freckled skin glowing with a sheen of sweat.

'Molly has agreed to be my maid of honour,' Zahara said, transferring her arms to her fiancée, her cheek hovering close to the sweat.

'Really?' Carolyn seemed as surprised by the news as Molly had been. 'Well, I can't think of anyone better for the job. I wish I felt my best woman had half the organising skills you have, Molly. My hen do was basically a gigantic pub crawl around Hoxton, ending up in a strip club in the West End. Complete nightmare.'

'Are you having a hen do?' Molly asked Zahara. 'Should I be organising that?'

'It's all organised. Daddy is letting us have his newest hotel suite in London, in a hotel he is just opening, and there will be a film crew there too. It will be so beautiful. The bridesmaids can do their dances. You can just let your hair down and be a guest like everyone else for one night.'

The designer of the wedding dress was also working on the bridesmaids' outfits that day. As she took Molly's measurements, half an hour later, Molly found herself surprisingly excited at the thought of having her body swathed in acres of soft, golden silk. It would be like dressing up as a princess, which she hadn't done since she was a small child.

CHAPTER TWENTY-FOUR

Molly had knocked on virtually every door in the village in order to log as many spare bedrooms as possible. She even noted down the spare room in her gran's cottage, which had not been aired for at least a decade, but would still provide another bed for a weary head at the end of a kitchen or security shift. It wasn't just the guests who were going to need more accommodation than the big house and the pub could provide, it was also the army of staff, including the actors, technicians, caterers, costumiers, make-up artists, and everyone else needed to create a few days of Bollywood/Hollywood/social media magic.

An encampment of army tents had been erected out of sight behind the stables for the key workers who needed to stay on site, including the growing battalion of security people, who were now required to keep watch over the whole village as the festivities loomed closer. Eight-foot-high fences now surrounded the house and gardens, within which the guests would be safely cocooned. Every corner was studded with security cameras, as well as the cameras installed by the television news and documentary companies. Several reporters and photographers had tried spending time in the pub in the hope of digging up background stories, but they found the villagers curiously protective of everyone involved in the big house. Eventually, they moved on to cluster outside the various gates, some of them watching over the whole estate from drones.

'It's a frigging invasion,' a voice in the pub spoke on behalf of many, when he was sure there were no strange faces within earshot, 'that's what it is. The whole village is being taken over.'

'Still,' a more moderate voice chimed in, 'Molly says I can get a hundred pounds a night for every guest I can give a bed to. I don't even have to provide breakfast. That's handy money.'

'Yeah,' another agreed, 'I've told the kids they'll have to sleep in with us for a few nights, to free up their beds.'

'Does your Molly think this sort of thing is going to be a regular occurrence then, Joanie?'

'I don't know,' Joan admitted, clearing glasses by the handful, 'but it could be a tidy little earner for the whole village if it is.'

'Turning our own houses into a camping site,' the dissenting voice resumed, 'saving them the expense of building anything.'

'It's not compulsory,' Joan snapped, 'just an option to make some easy cash, if you want to take it up.'

'It's the thin end of the wedge, if you ask me,' the dissenter muttered. 'They'll gradually take over everything, it'll all go out of our price range and we'll all be out on the street.'

'Who's they?' a younger voice challenged. 'Who are you feeling so threatened by?'

'The rich. They've got everything else in the world, so now they want to add us to their list of possessions.'

'Thank you, Karl Marx,' Joan sniffed.

'What have we got that they would want?' someone else asked. 'This place is hardly Paris, is it?'

'They need a ready supply of people to wait on them hand and foot. That's what they want. And they want to enjoy the unspoiled peace and quiet of village life, the very thing they will destroy once they take over. It's always the same. We'll all end up sweating for them in their kitchens, scrubbing their bathrooms, making their homes and gardens look like magazine covers. They'll pay us a few pounds here and there, but they'll end up owning the lot, and charging us rent for the privilege of living here. You mark my words.'

'That's the way of the world,' Joan said. 'Nothing much we can do about it. You need another drink to cheer yourself up, you miserable old git.'

'That I do, Joanie,' the dissenter agreed, 'that I do.'

. . .

First came the giant trucks, bearing tents and industrial kitchens, accompanied by buses full of men to erect them, inhabit them and guard them. Many of the builders and decorators were still at work putting the finishing touches to inside the house, while gardeners worked on amongst the electricians, who were filling the newly planted trees with several miles of fairy lights. Generators hummed constantly from behind the stables, so that the village was not drained by the power needed to keep the wheels turning on the whole show. A stage was erected for the star names, who were rumoured to have been paid seven-figure sums to perform, and crowned with a canopy modelled on the Sydney Opera House, just in case of rain. The lawns were covered with a network of raised, carpeted walkways, so that guests' heels would not sink into the freshly rolled grass. A flock of flamingos was introduced to the lake, causing the swans to form a defensive fighting force, requiring the zoo keeper and her assistant to keep watch twenty-four hours a day until the new pecking order had been finalised.

From the windows of the house, and from the lawns, nothing was visible to the guests except beauty and perfection in every direction. The cameras continued to follow every aspect of the construction and decoration, revelling in the vast costs being incurred and the levels of luxury that were achievable as a result. Zahara's followers were able to track her excitement almost all day long.

'I want every young girl in the world to be able to believe she can have the perfect wedding day,' she told everyone who would listen. 'You need to know that if you dream of being a princess then you have the right to do it. No one should be able to stop you. But you don't have to be a princess if you want something different. If you want to be a world-class sports person, then Carolyn is here to inspire you as well. This is a festival to celebrate the joys of individual choice. Every person in the world should be free to be whoever they want to be.'

Then came the actors, and the production team that had put together the various tableaux to mimic the photographs from Bryan's album. The uncanny likeness of the main player to the young Bryan she had once known made part of Mrs Woodcock want to hide inside her cottage and not come out until the entire production was over, while at the same time repeatedly drawing her out through the door, with a force as powerful as invisible bungee ropes, for just one more glimpse. The casting director had been given copies of the photographs and had been instructed to find a young man who 'could play Dorian Gray, before the portrait went into the attic'. After several weeks of searching, they had been forced to pay an enormous sum for a boy from Sweden, whose greatest claim to fame was appearing in a global advertising campaign for Burberry, and modelling on the catwalk for them in London and Milan. His resemblance to the pictures of Bryan at that age was so striking the producers had no option but to pay the exorbitant price demanded by his New York modelling agency. They were also required to provide him with his own Winnebago, which was parked alongside the ones hired for the less senior members of the wedding party to get dressed in and retire to for a rest should the festivities prove too much for them.

'Looks a lot like him,' Benson said, catching her staring at the young man, as he passed with a wheelbarrow full of compost for his garden, 'doesn't he?'

'Who? Do you think so? I hadn't noticed. Maybe. He never wore his hair like that, and he didn't have glasses until he was an old man ...' She stopped talking abruptly, blushing deeply when she saw that Benson was mocking her as he continued on his way without breaking his stride. She was sure she heard him chuckle in a tone that made her want to stab him in the back with his own garden fork.

CHAPTER TWENTY-FIVE

Molly heard the screams from inside the big house, where she had been having a morning meeting with the caterers. It sounded like they were coming from the walled garden, where she knew the seamstress and designer had gone to choose the roses they wanted picked later that evening, so they could be sewn onto the dress for the following day. The screaming and babble of raised voices did not stop.

'Excuse me,' she said to the meeting, 'I think I need to check this out.'

Other people were running in the same direction by the time she came outside, no one having any idea what the problem could be. She noticed Benson sitting on his deck-chair outside his cottage door, reading a book. He did not bother to look up. The hysterics of excitable young people were of no interest to him. Bryan, however, who had been stretched out at his feet in the sun, was fully alert to the drama and obviously longing to be given the all-clear to investigate. A small crowd had gathered at the far end of the walled garden, where Molly could see that the wedding dress team had already tied a few white ribbons onto blooms that they liked the look of and wanted to designate for harvesting at the last moment, before whatever calamity had struck.

'What's happened?' she demanded of the group.

'It is so gross!' the young seamstress was gabbling. 'It's like a nightmare!'

Molly moved closer to see what they were talking about and was unable to stop herself from exclaiming at the sight of Rotter's eyeless, fleshless remains, lying contorted on the twisted roots of the plum tree, drying in the sun, squirming with worms and other subterranean life forms.

'Okay,' she shouted over the noise, 'everybody back to the house. Turn off the cameras. Let me sort this out and I will let you know when it is safe to come back.'

Once she had herded everyone out of the walled garden, she called over a couple of the security team and asked them to keep guard over the gate until she returned.

Benson had obviously heard her approach, alerted by the welcoming thump of Bryan's tail against the dry ground, but he didn't look up from his book.

'Sorry to disturb you, Mr Benson,' Molly said, her voice quiet out of respect for the news she was about to impart. 'I'm afraid something rather unpleasant has happened.'

Benson finally looked up. 'I heard some screaming,' he said matter-of-factly.

'I'm afraid it's your dog.' Bryan pricked up his ears. 'Your old dog. The one you buried under the plum tree in the walled garden.'

'Rotter.'

'Sorry?'

'That was his name, Rotter.'

'Oh yes, of course. Sorry. Rotter. I'm afraid someone has dug him up. It's given everyone a bit of a shock.'

'Won't be a pretty sight after all this time,' he said. 'It'll be the foxes; they'll dig up anything they can find.'

'Would you like me to ask the security people to deal with it?' Molly asked.

'Nah.' He pulled himself up, dropping the book onto the faded stripes of the canvas chair. Molly noticed the title, *The Ballad of Reading Gaol*. 'I'll take care of it. I'll get my spade. I'll dig him in deeper this time, put something on top so they can't smell him.'

'Good book?' she asked as he walked away, unable to hide her curiosity, but he didn't look back.

CHAPTER TWENTY-SIX

The wedding party and their guests were the final pieces of Molly's logistical jigsaw. They arrived in a swarm of helicopters and convoys of limousines. Villagers who came out in the hope of spotting celebrities were disappointed to find that they recognised hardly anyone amongst Vijay's billionaire business acquaintances and the many international politicians who had benefited over the years from his donations. The British prime minister received some half-hearted jeers from the few people who recognised him as he climbed out of his car, waving cheerfully at anyone pointing a camera in his direction, and quite a few who weren't even looking in his direction, but the more widely recognisable faces, such as actors and singers, were spirited invisibly in through different entrances by the army of security people that was now assembled all around the perimeter.

The younger villagers were able to show the others how to live-stream what was happening behind the newly erected screens of young silver birch trees and security fencing, on Zahara's social feeds. There was a ripple of excitement every time they spotted Molly in the background, looking more beautiful than most of them had ever noticed in a gold sari and a professionally applied mask of make-up, moving around the crowd, ensuring that everything was running smoothly. The cameras gave almost as much time to the otherworldly beauty of the actor who was posing as the young Bryan from the photographs as they did to Zahara and Carolyn.

A lot of viewers were also surprised by just how beautiful Carolyn was when the mud and sweat of the football pitch were wiped away by skilful hairdressers and make-up artists, and the perfection of the rose blossoms stitched to Zahara's dress meant that wherever she went in the wedding compound, she was surrounded by seething clusters of photographers who had outlets in the fashion press, which had allowed them to apply for 'access all areas' passes.

Not wishing to be noticed, but unable to resist the sugary lure of the glamorous wealth on display, Mrs Woodcock was watching on the phone Zahara had given her, from the privacy of her own kitchen. Feeling an overwhelming urge to share the experience of seeing a young Bryan haunting the lawns and terraces of his ancestral home at least one more time, she took the phone over to Benson's cottage, finding him sitting at his kitchen table, reading. He didn't look as displeased to see her as she had expected.

'Hiding?' she asked.

'Reading,' he replied, surprised that she didn't tut, as she usually did when she caught him 'wasting time' on books.

She pulled up a chair and sat down beside him, propping the phone up against a pile of paperbacks so that they could both watch.

'Did you hear the commotion earlier?' she asked. 'With the flamingos?'

'Yeah,' he chuckled. 'Foxes got them. Could have told them that would happen. Stupid birds were just standing there, fast asleep on one leg, heads stuck under their wings. Not exactly hard for a fox to take them by surprise.'

'There were feathers everywhere.'

'A killing spree.' He chuckled again.

'Have you seen the actor, now they've got him dressed up as Bryan?' she asked.

Benson said nothing, but leant forward for a closer look at the screen.

'That one,' she said. 'See? They've put him in exactly the same clothes, and changed his hair.'

'Bugger me,' Benson said.

'I know. It's uncanny, don't you think?'

They watched together in silence for several minutes, before Bryan woke them from their reveries by barking at the sound of footsteps approaching fast. There was a light knock. Benson ordered Bryan to sit back down and opened the door. Mrs Woodcock recognised the upright woman in the black business suit who always seemed to follow Zahara's father around like a shadow. There was something deeply untrustworthy about her, like she was a hologram rather than a real person, an immaculate product of artificial intelligence.

'Ah, Mrs Woodcock.' Charu seemed to know who she was, which surprised her. 'I'm glad I found you. I was going to suggest that I should talk to you both together.'

They could hear the live music and laughter drifting across the lawns as well as from the phone screen. Charu's heels clicked across the ancient tiles of the kitchen floor and she snapped two pristine business cards down on the table in front of them.

'My name is Charu and I am the legal representative of Zahara's father, Vijay.'

They both stared at the cards for a moment, uneasy as to why this woman would have taken time away from the festivities to seek them out. It felt like a visit from some sort of beautiful, dead-eyed harbinger of doom. Benson remembered Daisy's warning words.

'May I sit down?' She didn't wait for a reply before joining them, her elegant hands resting on the table in front of her, as if to demonstrate she had nothing to hide, no tricks up her sleeve. Mrs Woodcock silenced the sound of the festivities still emanating from the phone, leaving them as a distant hum through the thick cottage walls, and they both straightened up in their chairs, as if they were children about to be addressed by a strict teacher, unsure if they were in trouble or not. Benson relit his cigarette stub in a small gesture of rebellion against the clean fragrance of their visitor's perfume.

'I expect you know that Vijay's company now owns the house and what is left of the estate,' she said, and neither of them blinked. 'We have some very exciting plans for developing it into a really beautiful, exclusive hotel and wedding venue. I expect you have seen the designers around the place in recent months, measuring up, working out how to make it the best it can possibly be.'

Still they did not respond, but their silence did not seem to intimidate her in the least. Charu was used to face-offs and tough negotiations. She was a champion poker player in what spare time Vijay's demanding schedule allowed her.

'Part of the plan would be to utilise every part of the property to its maximum advantage. We would really love to modernise this cottage, and your cottage, Mrs Woodcock. They both have such old-world charm, but obviously they have not had anything done to them for many, many years. They are badly in need of updating.'

Charu thought she saw them exchange the slightest of warning glances, as if they sensed danger. But then the moment passed and she wasn't sure if she had imagined it, and still neither of them spoke.

'Vijay would like to make you both an offer. He would like to offer you each a hundred thousand pounds, and then he would arrange for a loan if you wanted to buy another property in the area, something that requires less maintenance, perhaps. A serviced apartment, maybe.' She paused for a few seconds more of silence. 'It would save you both the disruption of having the cottages renovated around you.'

Their lack of response was beginning to make her unsure how to proceed. This was not how these sorts of negotiations usually went, in her experience. She had expected to see some fear in their eyes, maybe some anger and defensive behaviour. Or maybe a flicker of greed or opportunism. She was well trained in how to exploit all those emotions in the course of a negotiation. This wall of silence was a new experience for her. It was more like facing them over a poker table. She told herself that she must learn from it, so that next time she would have a response ready, and never be caught out this way again.

'I'll leave you two to think it over,' she said, standing up. 'Talk it through and let me know what you decide. Give me a call.' She gestured towards the business cards, still lying untouched on the table, before letting herself out the door, allowing a gust of music in before closing it behind her. Bryan watched her go with pricked ears.

Without asking, Benson stood up and made them coffees, just as he used to do for Bryan. He knew she wouldn't drink it, but he couldn't be bothered to put the kettle on for tea and he wanted something to do with his hands while he thought.

'This will just be the start,' he said, sitting back down with the cups, 'you know that? The French woman told me this would happen. They've finished with us. We're no longer of any use to them.'

'Who has finished with us?'

'All of them. The rich. The owners. The people we have been saying "yes, sir" and "no, sir" to all our lives.'

'Haven't heard you doing much of that lately.'

'Maybe that's another reason they no longer have any use for us,' Benson said. 'Have you seen how eager all the young people around here are to please the people they are working for? The celebrities? The ones who swan around in helicopters. The ones who need their arses licking in order to survive, even though they haven't done anything to earn it.'

'They've earned the money that buys it,' Mrs Woodcock said.

'They certainly have the money. Don't know that I would say they have exactly earned it. If they had earned it, I might be more inclined to doff my cap to them.'

'Haven't seen you doff your cap since you were ten years old and your father gave you that clip round the ear for not saying good morning to the Colonel when he was riding past.'

'Yeah.' Benson allowed himself a smile. 'I dare say you're right there. Bryan used to say that we had reached the end of the age of deference, but I don't think we have. Now people just defer to a different kind of person. They still bow and curtsy to the royals, and chase the celebrities around with their cameras and their autograph books. Have you seen how many security staff they have to have around an event like this? It's like a private army, there to protect them from being torn to pieces by the mob. It's like *The Day of the Locust* has arrived.'

'You read too many books,' Mrs Woodcock replied. 'Always have. It gives you too many funny ideas.'

'So you say, but you still know I'm right.'

'I've had enough,' Mrs Woodcock said after a few moments of thought. 'I'm tired of the whole business.'

'What's the whole business then?'

'All this—' she gestured out the window towards the swirling mass of glittery people across the lawn '—nonsense.'

'I wouldn't want to leave here,' Benson said, looking round at the room he had spent so much of his life in.

'They won't give us any peace till they have us out,' she said.

'I know. That's what the French woman said.'

'I've had enough,' she repeated. 'Someone else can polish all those damn floors now. Not me.'

'They won't do anything to help us,' Benson said, 'we both know that. Not once they've got what they want. Once they've got us out of here, it'll be the scrap-heap for us.'

She nodded, surprised to find that she didn't even feel that sad, just tired. In fact, she felt a kind of relief, as if she had reached the end of a long ordeal. It was the same feeling she had experienced when Bryan had finally stopped breathing. She wasn't a religious woman. She didn't believe that she would be reunited with Bryan on the other side, or anything like that, but she didn't relish the idea of continuing with a life without any hope of ever seeing him again either.

'I don't know how to work that thing,' she said, pointing to the shotgun resting against the wall in the corner of the room. 'Otherwise, I would use it.'

'I'm meant to have that under lock and key,' Benson said absent-mindedly.

'Would you show me how to use it?' she asked. 'I've had enough.'

Bryan seemed to be listening, following their conversation like a tennis match, panting a little anxiously as Benson stood up and walked stiffly to the gun. He stroked it thoughtfully. 'You want to end it?'

'I think so. I've had enough.'

'I'll help you. If you're sure.'

'You could be done for murder. You don't want to end your days in jail.'

'I'll come with you,' he said. 'We'll go together.'

'Like a brother and sister?' she chuckled.

'Don't start all that again,' he said, jiggling the ammunition casually in the palm of his hand. 'No one will hear us over that racket.'

'How would you do it?'

He shrugged, looking round the room. 'Sit you comfortably in the armchair,' he suggested. 'Hold a cushion over your face and pull the trigger. Then I'll follow you.'

'What about the dog? I don't want to end up being dog food.'

'I'll open the door for him, so he can get out when he's ready.'

Benson stood, with the gun held loosely in his hand, waiting for her to speak. Bryan continued to watch both of them, his tail a slow, uncertain accompanying drumbeat on the floor.

'Yes,' she said eventually. 'I think it would be a good time to draw a line under the whole business. Let's not prolong the agony by discussing it anymore. We will just be going round in circles. Do it.'

It sounded like the sort of dare she would have set him when they were eight or nine years old, when he had always felt compelled to follow her lead in whatever plan she had concocted for them, whether it was running across thin ice on the lake, climbing the highest trees in the woods, putting ferrets down his trousers or eating worms.

They said nothing more, avoiding looking into one another's eyes as she plumped herself into the armchair and lifted the cushion over her face and he loaded the gun. He did not hesitate, any more than he would have hesitated to pull the trigger when his sights were lined up on a fat pigeon or a grazing rabbit. He held the barrel less than an inch from the cushion and fired. The noise filled the kitchen and Bryan let out a howl of surprise as he sprang to his feet, running to rest his chin in Mrs Woodcock's lap, letting out a whimper of distress, which Benson didn't hear over the ringing in his ears. He did not look at the cushion, knowing what he would see if he did. He walked quickly to the door and opened it enough for Bryan to be able to leave easily, sat down on one of the kitchen chairs and turned the second barrel on himself.

A few people at the party heard the two explosions, and wondered out loud if they were missing out on fireworks in another part of the estate. It would be several hours before the team manning the security cameras noticed the Alsatian, glowing eerily white in the ultraviolet lights of the dance floor, trotting amongst the gyrating crowd, searching for something he would never find. Only when they caught him and took him into a brightly lit tent did they realise that the marks around his muzzle, which had appeared black in the dance floor lights, were actually blood red.

CHAPTER TWENTY-SEVEN

'May I sit here?' Daisy asked.

'Of course,' Joan replied, sliding along the already packed pew to free up enough room, forcing her neighbour's elderly Labrador to rise from his slumbers at her feet. He rested his chin on her lap and gazed reproachfully up at her. 'Lucky you are so slim.'

Daisy smiled politely at the compliment. 'It was hard to get in through the crowd,' she said.

'Bit of a scrum,' Joan agreed, absent-mindedly stroking the dog's head as his eyelids drooped shut once more.

'I have been to a few funerals lately,' Daisy said, 'I am of that age.' She shrugged, as if to reassure Joan that aging did not worry her. 'But I have never seen anything like this. And some of my friends were very famous once.'

'I think you could call it a media feeding frenzy.'

The vicar had made it very clear that no cameras would be allowed inside the church for the ceremony, apart from the ones making the documentary for Zahara, and even they had been required to make a substantial contribution to the church restoration fund before he would grant permission. The result was that the path to the church door from the gate was entirely lined with news cameras and photographers, all shouting questions over the barriers at the villagers who were making their way to the service, mostly out of curiosity. They didn't even fall silent when the two coffins passed by on the shoulders of professional pall-bearers. As Zahara appeared behind them, dramatically veiled and discreetly filming on her phone, the roar of shouted questions intensified. She did not turn her head, confident that her bodyguard was following, eyes darting everywhere from behind his dark glasses. She left her camera running as she found her reserved seat, despite the vicar's edict and despite having received warning letters from the documentary-makers' lawyers. Two seats away from her, an editor from the publisher who had submitted the highest bid for her autobiography gave a little wave, wanting to be sure that Zahara had seen she had made the effort to travel all the way up from London to support her in her grief. Zahara nodded a response, her expression invisible behind the veil.

The vicar was obviously flustered, never having faced such a packed congregation, all of whom he knew were hoping for some new drama to occur. He was painfully aware he had nothing of interest to say to them. All he knew about the deceased was whatever he had heard about them in the pub. He had been in the bar on the night they emerged from the big house to announce the death of their employer, but he hadn't run across them again. He was just going to have to deliver a few standard words about them living simple, unpretentious lives of selfless service to others.

In the end, his words were drowned out by the shouts of the media outside anyway.

. . .

As they left the church, and the gauntlet of cameras, behind them, Joan found Daisy walking beside her.

'How is your mother?' Daisy asked.

'I was just on my way to see her,' Joan said. 'Would you like to come? She told Molly that she remembers your mother.'

'I would very much like to meet her,' Daisy said.

Alice's carer was just leaving as they arrived at the cottage, having got her up, dressed, breakfasted and made her comfortable in her chair beside the Aga.

'Morning, Mum,' Joan greeted her cheerily, 'I've brought someone to see you. This is Daisy.'

'Good morning.' Daisy stepped forward so the old woman could get a clear view. 'I am Claudette's daughter.'

'Do you remember Claudette, Mum?' Joan asked. 'A French girl who worked up at the big house.'

'You're the spitting image of her,' Alice said. 'Although she was a lot younger.'

'Yes,' Daisy agreed, 'I think she was only in her early twenties.'

'She would have been the same age as me,' Alice said. 'I'm ninety.'

'Yes, that would have been right. My mother has passed away, I'm afraid, but she would be ninety now if she was alive.'

'Everyone has passed away now. I won't be long for this world.'

'You've got a few good years in you yet, Mum,' Joan said, more out of habit than conviction.

'She had to go back to France, you know,' Alice said. 'Your mother.'

'Yes,' Daisy replied, sitting herself down next to the old woman. 'That's right.'

'I dare say it was because you were on the way.'

'Yes, I believe so.'

'She's a good girl, you know.'

'Who is a good girl?'

'My Joanie.' Alice nodded towards her daughter, who appeared to be engrossed in her phone and not listening. 'She's the one who stayed in the village and looked after me. Her brother and sister, I never see them anymore.'

'That's not quite true, Mum,' Joan said, without looking up from her screen. 'They come when they can, but they both live a long way away.'

'I never thought Joanie would be the one who would stay and look after me,' Alice continued, as if her daughter hadn't spoken. 'I remember your mother. He brought her back from France with him, after the war.'

'I think she looked after the horses for him,' Daisy prompted.

Alice pursed her already shrunken lips. 'She was a pretty little thing. Didn't know any better, I dare say. It's nice to see you two getting on.'

Joan looked up from her screen. 'Daisy is staying at the pub, Mum. I just thought you would like to meet her.'

Alice squinted hard at her daughter and then refocused her gaze on Daisy. 'I can see a resemblance. You've both a look of him. He was a handsome old bastard, I'll give him that.'

Daisy sat back in her seat and watched the dawning realisation spreading across Joan's face.

They let Alice talk a bit longer. Joan made a pot of tea and she and Daisy stole the odd glance at one another as they listened, occasionally volunteering comments of their own. The conversation made progressively less sense as the old woman grew weary and her eyelids began to droop.

'We're going to leave you now, Mum,' Joan said, 'to have a little sleep. I'll get Molly to drop in later, before she heads back to London.'

'All right, lovey,' Alice said, allowing her lids to close as they made their way out.

Walking back down the high street, towards the pub, neither of the women spoke. After about fifty yards, however, Joan felt Daisy's black-gloved fingers slipping into hers, and she returned the squeeze as they strolled on.

ABOUT THE AUTHOR

Andrew Crofts has published more than a hundred books, many of which have become international bestsellers. At one stage, he had four books in the *Sunday Times* bestseller list simultaneously.

He has ghostwritten on a wide range of subjects, from the rulers of countries to a survivor of the Rwandan genocide, a child bride in the Yemen and a refugee from South Sudan, plus winners of reality TV shows, pop stars, hairdressers, bonded labourers and sex workers.

He has been a prize on the *Richard and Judy Show*, a birthday gift for an Asian billionaire and the muse for Robert Harris's thriller *The Ghost*, which Roman Polanski turned into a film with Ewan McGregor as the ghostwriter and Pierce Brosnan as the Tony Blair figure.

His books on writing include *Ghostwriting* (A&C Black) and *The Freelance Writer's Handbook* (Piatkus), which has been reprinted eight times over twenty years, and *Confessions of a Ghostwriter* (Friday Project).

Andrew also writes his own thrillers; most recently *What Lies Around Us* and *Secrets of the Italian Gardener*, which feature a ghostwriter as the main protagonist.